Stacey

Stacey

Eileen Pollinger

BETHANY HOUSE PUBLISHERS
MINNEAPOLIS, MINNESOTA 55438
A Division of Bethany Fellowship, Inc.

Stacey
Eileen Pollinger

Library of Congress Catalog Card Number 87–71604
ISBN 0–87123–943–4

Published by Bethany House Publishers
A Division of Bethany Fellowship, Inc.
6820 Auto Club Road, Minneapolis, Minnesota 55438

Printed in the United States of America

EILEEN POLLINGER is a graduate of Montana State University and has authored articles for *Decision* magazine. She is active in the Washington Christian Writer's Fellowship and the Seattle Pacific University Writer's Conference. She is married and lives in Snohomish, Washington. This is her second book.

Chapter One

"Stacey Carolyn White."

Stacey crossed the stage as the principal called her name, happy with her decision to go by her first name, instead of her middle name. The change symbolized to her the changes she hoped would take place in her life now that she was graduating from high school.

She focused less on receiving her diploma than on searching the audience to see if her father had made it for her graduation. Bitterness rankled. His job seemed to take him away from home during all the major events of her life.

None of her brothers or her sister had even considered coming. Only her mother would be here for sure. She had promised to sit in a certain section, and Stacey searched that area. If her mother was alone, she probably wouldn't find her. She had the kind of dull looks that disappear in a crowd.

Then she spotted a man with black hair winged with silver at the temples. Her father. Joy and delight straightened her shoulders and lent lightness to her step.

She shook hands with the principal and received her diploma from the school superintendent. Gold honor braid swung from the shoulder of her white gown with each gesture.

Moving her tassel from left to right, she again sought out her father's face in the audience. His nod of approval and slight smile were all she needed to make the evening perfect. Well, almost.

Stacey wished—oh, how she wished—she had friends who cared more about her. Last night, when her dad had called to say he might make it home in time for the ceremony, she'd phoned her only true friend, a girl who'd graduated the year before.

"Becky?"

"Yes?"

"This is Stacey. Guess what! Dad just called and said he might be able to fly in late tomorrow. He can only stay a day or two, so if he comes, I won't be going to the church graduation party with you tomorrow night."

"That's wonderful!" Becky chuckled. "That your dad might come home, I mean. I know how much you want him to be here. We'll miss you, but you need to spend the time with your dad. See you next Sunday?"

"Probably. Unless I talk Dad into taking me with him for the summer."

"Oh, Carolyn—I mean *Stacey*—I'll never get used to calling you by your first name . . . Can you?"

"I'm going to try."

"Great. Sorry I have to rush, but my dad's taken a turn for the worse. I promised Mom I'd make sure the kids get ready for school tomorrow."

"Is your dad still taking radiation treatments?"

"No, he's supposed to be in a holding pattern right now. But he may have to start again."

"I'm sorry. I know they're tough. Does that mean you won't be at graduation tomorrow night?"

"No, I'll be there. My sister Dondra is playing in the orchestra. I told Mom I'll take her. I'll be there, cheering for you and the others."

It would have been nice if Becky had tried to persuade her to attend the party or to stick around for the summer, Stacey thought as she marched down the steps. She took her place in the row and sat down. She shrugged. Perhaps it was just as well. She hadn't really been looking forward to the party anyway.

Erica would undoubtedly be there with Mike. And Stacey had reason not to want to be around Erica. She'd avoided her for the past month, feeling guilty and wanting to apologize, but not quite having the courage.

She shook the unpleasant thoughts away, her glossy black hair gleaming in the light. This was her big night. She'd graduated with honors, and Dad was here to help her celebrate.

She listened to the last few moments of the ceremony, stood with the rest of the students, and flung her cap into the air. She caught it neatly and headed for her parents, returning her dad's hug with all her strength. "That's my little Stacey girl," he whispered.

Then her mother hugged her. Stacey allowed the hug, but didn't respond.

"Hurry now, dear," her mother urged. "Check in your cap and gown so we can be on our way. I told my supervisor I'd be at the hospital by ten. I don't want to be late." Her mother's light brown hair was already pulled back in the tight bun she wore under her nurse's cap.

Her father softened the nagging command with a wink. "And you and I don't want to be late for the dinner reservation I made at Le Napoleon."

Stacey smiled at him, transforming her face from sullen prettiness to radiant beauty. "I'll be back in two shakes of your old lamb's tail," she called over her shoulder. "Don't disappear."

She felt another twinge of guilt at how happy she'd been that her mother hadn't wanted to try to change her shift at the hospital when her father's coming was only a possibility. This way she'd have her dad all to herself at their celebration dinner, giving her a better chance to persuade him to take her with him.

She slipped out of her graduation robe, revealing a beautifully draped white sheer wool dress. She tapped the toe of her white high-heeled pump impatiently as she waited in line to return her cap and gown. Conversation, congratulations, cat calls, and friendly teasing flowed around her. Stacey paid no attention. She had few friends in this crowd.

Her turn came, and she deposited robe and cap on the heap on the table. As she turned to leave the room, she heard her name.

"Stacey!"

Reluctantly, she looked around. "Yes?"

"I thought I'd miss you," panted Erica. "You are coming to the party, aren't you?"

"Can't make it. Something came up." Stacey's voice was almost harsh. Why couldn't she just blurt out an apology and get over being so uncomfortable around Erica?

"Oh . . . sorry . . . Maybe we'll see each other this summer. Bye."

Stacey paused before she went through the door. Erica sounded as if she really meant it. Maybe . . . She shook back her silky black hair and went to meet her father. What did the Ericas of the world matter when she had a dinner date with her dad?

As she met her parents in the lobby, Becky came dashing up. "Congratulations," she said, giving Stacey a hug. "I didn't know you were graduating with honors. I'm impressed."

"Thanks." Stacey smiled warmly. "Do you know my parents? Dad, this is Becky James, my friend. Mom."

Becky's brown eyes sparkled as she acknowledged the introductions. "It's nice to meet you." She touched Stacey's arm. "Have a good time. I'm glad your dad made it."

Stacey shook her head warningly. She crossed her fingers, hoping Becky wouldn't mention her plan to talk her dad into taking her to Colorado.

She didn't. "I hate to run, but I've got to take Dondra over to the church and then get home."

"How is your father?" Stacey asked.

"A little better tonight, but I can't leave Mom alone too

long. It's hard for her to keep the younger kids quiet and concentrate on Dad at the same time."

"Carolyn—*Stacey*, we really must go," Mrs. White interrupted. She smiled at Becky. "I have to be at the hospital soon, and I don't want to be late."

"I'll call you tomorrow," Stacey promised over her shoulder, following her parents out the door.

They dropped Mrs. White off at the house to change into her uniform and headed for the little French restaurant. Le Napoleon, once a private home, was partially surrounded by a tall board fence. The exterior, shabby and painted a sickly blue, wasn't in the least appealing, but the food and service were superb.

Stacey looked up from her menu at her dad. She was glad she'd inherited his black hair instead of her mother's mousy brown, now streaked with gray. She only wished her eyes were as deeply blue as his. Still, they weren't as pale as her mother's.

Gazing at the silvery gray over her father's temples, Stacey wondered if she would some day have that sophisticated look. Would she be as immersed in life when she was sixty?

He looked up. "Made your decision?"

"Yes. I've decided to let you order for me. I love everything on the menu, and it's hard to choose which one I want tonight." His smile warmed her heart. "Besides, I feel special when you choose what you think I'll like best."

"You are special, Stacey. Special to both your mother and me."

A scowl twisted Stacey's face. "I don't think I'm so special to Mom. In fact, most of the time, I think I'm an intrusion, someone who came along nine years after the others to cause her trouble."

"Carolyn!" His use of that name conveyed both hurt and reprimand. His favorite name for her had always been Stacey. "True, you weren't planned, but we were both delighted when we knew you were on the way. We've never regretted having you."

"Then why . . ."

The waiter came, and Mr. White ordered. "We'll have the *Soupe du jour* and *Salade Verte Mimosa*. Then my daughter would like *Les Aiguillettes de Canard aux Dommes* and I'll have *Le Carred Agneau aux herbes*."

The waiter bowed and hurried off to the kitchen. Mr. White searched Stacey's eyes. "Why what?"

"Why does she treat me so differently?"

"What do you mean?"

"She had rules and deadlines and chores and things for Sandra and the boys." Stacey's eyes dropped, then met her father's again.

"The same rules apply to you."

She shook her head.

The waiter brought the soup and set it before them. "Anything to drink now?" he asked.

"Ice water, please. We'll have coffee later." Mr. White allowed the waiter to fill their glasses before he continued. "What seems to be different?"

"It's . . . oh, let's not talk about it now. We'll ruin our celebration dinner. Tell me about you. What are you working on now?" Her father, a nuclear physicist, worked from time to time on special projects for the government.

"Sorry, Stacey. I can't discuss it. This one's hush-hush."

"When will you be finished?"

"We hoped to be done by September, but things haven't been going well the last couple of months. It may extend on into the fall."

After the waiter served Stacey's breast of duckling and Mr. White's rack of lamb, Stacey ventured, "I'd like to ask a favor, Dad."

"And that is?"

"I'd like to spend the summer with you." She rushed on before he could answer. "I know I wouldn't be much help in the lab, but I could learn and I wouldn't be in the way. I promise."

"I'm sorry, Stacey. I can't."

"Please, Dad? It'd give me a head start for college."

"No. The secrecy classification of this project is too high to allow you to join me. I don't have the authority to include you."

"Could I just go along and sort of take care of you? I could cook and wash and stuff."

"Sorry, Stacey, that's not possible either. We're living in a compound with everything provided for us. Besides, we work long hours and I'd have no time to spend with you. I'm just too busy."

"I understand." Stacey didn't try to hide her disappointment. "I should have known it wouldn't work. Nothing I want ever does."

"Oh, come now. You'll be busy with friends, planning your clothes for college this fall, dating." He smiled at her. "Speaking of dating, what happened to that young man you wrote about? Mike, was it?"

"Mike? He's going with Erica Nelson now."

"Nelson? The daughter of the owner of the Kerusso? Didn't he get his newspaper in a lot of trouble for slander?"

Stacey blushed as she remembered the part she'd played in strengthening that rumor. Anger riled, too, at the memory of how she'd been used, but she only said, "No. It proved to be a false accusation. A guy named Tyson did the slandering, and he's up for trial in a month or so."

"Is this Erica a friend of yours?"

"I know her. She graduated tonight, too, but we're not really friends." *Could we be?* Stacey wondered. Would Erica forgive her as Becky had promised she would?

"Is there any other special guy right now?"

"Not really. Oh, I'm dating a few guys, but no one important enough to tell you about."

They lingered over cups of rich, black coffee, talking about college and the courses Stacey planned to take the first year. After a while her father became distracted, and was having to make a visible effort to concentrate on their conversation. *It's always this way*, she thought. *He's interested only for so long and then something happens.*

Her earlier excitement faded completely. Nothing was working out the way she'd anticipated. He was so wrapped up in this project—at least that's what she assumed was on his mind—that he wasn't paying attention to her anymore. He'd retreated into himself as he often did when he was in the middle of solving a difficult problem.

When the waiter returned with their change, Stacey laid her napkin on the table and forced a smile. "I guess that ends our evening."

Did her father sigh in relief? "Guess so," he replied. "Ready?"

It was after midnight when they arrived home. Stacey hugged her father good night, then ran to her room. She slipped off her wool dress and let it fall in a heap at the foot of her bed, along with the rest of the clothes she'd worn that week.

Choking back tears, she snuggled into bed. Then disappointment overwhelmed her. Would things ever work out?

The next day and evening flew by, and her dad had to leave. Before Stacey was ready, her dad came to her room. "Time to go," he said.

"Isn't it a little early?"

"I'd like to take time to stop by the hospital on the way to the airport. I want to say good-bye to your mother." He sighed. "These quick trips are almost harder than not coming home at all. I'm reminded of all I'm missing by not being here."

"I know . . ." She forced a smile. "A touch of lipstick and I'll be ready to go."

Leaning forward to stroke on the lip color, Stacey caught the reflection of her dad in the mirror. His mouth tightened and he shook his head, looking at the mess strewn around her room. She expected a lecture, but he only said, "I am amazed that someone as fastidiously beautiful as you can emerge from such surroundings."

"I'll take care of it tomorrow," Stacey promised.

Passengers were already boarding when they arrived at the gate at SeaTac Airport. Two men in gray business suits stood off to one side, talking rapidly and tensely. Stacey saw her father's eyes flick toward them. She noticed a startled recognition followed by what? Anger? Fear? The look passed so quickly, Stacey couldn't be sure.

Her father turned his back on them and muttered, "I should have come by shuttle bus. I didn't dream—" He stopped, then added urgently, "Hurry home, Stacey. Remember, it's still unwise to talk to strangers." He patted her shoulder and was gone, waving as he disappeared down the jetway.

The two men stared at Stacey. The taller and younger of the two took a step toward her. The shorter, almost bald man grabbed his arm and held him back. After a few fierce words which Stacey couldn't hear, he released his grip and sprinted for the jetway.

Feeling a strange unease caused by her father's words and the stares of the two men, Stacey mingled with a large family who'd tearfully sent off one of their teenagers. She stayed with them until she approached the underground rail car that would take her to the main terminal. She ran to squeeze in just before the doors slid closed and before the curly-haired stranger in the gray suit could make it.

Safe in her dad's car, she laughed at herself. This wasn't the first time a handsome young man had stared at her—or ugly bald ones either. By the time she got home, she'd forgotten both of them, her thoughts turning to plans for the next day.

Before climbing into bed, she searched through the piles of papers and books on her desk and shelves until she found a well-worn book. She propped it against the powerful binoculars that had been her eighteenth birthday gift from her parents. She dug out a pair of worn jeans, a faded blue shirt and blue knee-high socks. She stacked them on a chair by the door and set her alarm for three-thirty.

Chapter Two

At four the next morning, Stacey stuffed stale bread in one pocket of her denim jacket and cheese and a banana in the other.

While she was still in the kitchen, her mother came in from work at the hospital. "Where are you going at this hour of the morning?"

Stacy nodded to *A Field Guide to Western Birds* lying with her binoculars on the table. "Bird watching."

"Oh, okay. Be sure you clean your room today."

Stacey caught up the book with its waterproof cover and attached pencil, slung the binoculars around her neck and raced out the back door without answering.

She'd clean her room today, but not because of her mother's nagging. Her father's quiet hint at the mess had been a powerful prod.

Sliding behind the wheel of her father's old Chevy, she headed south of town. A large wooded area about five miles out might shelter a flock of *psaltriparus minimus,* an elusive little bird she privately called mini's. She had yet to add them to her "life list" of birds she identified.

She parked the car at the end of Sixty-fifth Avenue and locked it, then walked through the woods until she found just the right mix of tall trees and low growing bushes. Wending her way through salmonberry bushes, prickly wild blackberry, and lacy huckleberry, she passed towering alder and hemlock and found a spot under an enormous cedar tree. She burrowed a resting place and stretched out on her stomach.

Deciding it would be comfortable enough for an extended wait, she left her book and glasses, and moved quietly, spreading crumbs and crusts of the dried bread in a large semi-circle around her cedar. Then she retreated under the tree and settled down to wait.

She listened for a while, identifying the calls of robins, juncos, and finches. Occasionally she lifted the binoculars to her eyes, scanning the area.

A brown creeper circled his way up a nearby tree trunk, and a flock of black-capped chickadees fluttered, hanging and twisting in acrobatic feats a circus performer would envy. A varied thrush thrashed its way through the twigs and debris on the forest floor searching for tidbits. Even a cautious rabbit came to sample the new food supply.

Relaxed in the soft debris under the tree, she dozed for a while. The early sun glinted through the woods as she woke to the distinctive tsit's and lisp's that made up the steady conversation of her quarry. She lifted her binoculars.

The tiny birds were often hard to spot as they flitted from bush to bush. She hadn't found them yet when she heard a different whistle—*The Skater's Waltz*, slightly off key—accompanied by the crashing of a body through the underbrush behind her and the swift departure of all the birds.

She twisted to see the intruder. A tall, blond young man knelt about twenty feet from her, now whistling at a more subdued volume as he set up a camera on a tripod.

"You might as well not bother," she snapped.

The young man jumped. He looked around and failed to see Stacey lying under the branches of the cedar. "Who's there?" he asked.

"No one. You've scared them all away with your stupid noise and crashing. So I may as well go, too." Stacey snatched up her guidebook and glasses and crawled out from under the low-slung branches. "Thanks for ruining my morning."

She turned to stride off, but the stranger called. "Hey, calm down. I'll be set up in three minutes. They'll all be back."

"Not the ones I was after."

"Oh, come on. You must have disturbed things for a time when you arrived. Settle back down. I won't make another sound." Gray-green eyes smiled down at her. "Promise."

She almost smiled back at him, wavered, then some inner decision clicked without her conscious volition. Anger surged. "Do you come here often?" she demanded.

"I'm fairly new to this area, but I shoot pictures two or three mornings a week."

"Right here?"

"Round about."

"Fine. Then I'll set up as far away as I can get."

"Look. If you can't share a quiet spot—"

"Quiet . . . until you arrived."

"I'll go. I'll find another place."

"Forget it. You've already ruined the morning," Stacey snapped and strode off through the woods.

At home, she stepped out of the dusty jeans and jacket and dropped them on the floor with her shirt. Taking a scarlet robe from the closet, she wrapped it around her. She flopped on the unmade bed and curled into a ball to sleep.

Her mother woke her shortly after noon. "Now that you're not in school, I thought the least you'd do is have a bite ready for me to eat when I woke up. Is that expecting too much?"

"Yes. Why should I? This is my vacation. Besides, I didn't have as much sleep as you. I went bird watching, remember?"

"Oh, of course." Her mother sighed. "I'll get lunch. What do you want?"

"Whatever you fix. I'm not hungry."

Stacey turned over onto her back while her mother bent to pick up the banana and cheese Stacey had left on top of her pile of clothes. She wished that just once her mother would stand up to her, would refuse to take the back talk she'd never have allowed from the older kids.

She closed her eyes to shut out the almost hopeless look on her mother's face. The door clicked shut, and Stacey opened her eyes to let out the tears she'd been holding escape. She shook her head angrily. Why should she cry? No one cared anyway.

When her mother called her for lunch, she retied the robe belt, dashed cold water on her face, stepped into matching red slippers and walked slowly downstairs.

Lunch was a silent, uncomfortable meal. While Mrs. White picked up the dishes to put them in the dishwasher she asked, "Would you like to go grocery shopping with me this afternoon?"

"No thanks. I need to do my hair and nails."

"Are you going out this evening?"

"I don't know. Maybe."

"Stacey." Pain laced her mother's voice and shadowed her eyes. "Don't make things worse than they are. It won't hurt you to be civil."

"I am. I don't know if I'm going out. Perhaps something will come up. If it does, I'll go."

"Of course," replied her mother, rinsing dishes at the sink. "Don't forget to clean your room."

"Don't worry about it."

Stacey ran up to her room. Why did her mother always bring out the worst in her? She determined so many times to be nice, to say the right things, but something about her mother—was it fear? or uncertainty? Whatever it was, it evoked irritation and grudging answers.

It was as if she were challenging her mother to be a mother—and Mother never took the challenge. She always backed down. She'd never been that way with the others that Stacey could remember. Why with her?

She flinched away from possible answers, dropped the robe across the bed and pulled on a pair of designer jeans and a blue cotton tee shirt. For a moment she almost decided to skip cleaning her room because her mom had mentioned it again. But she remembered the look on her dad's face the night before and plunged in.

She hauled all the dirty clothes piled on the floor to the laundry room, sorted them, and started to wash. Back in her room, she cleaned her desk and dresser, made the bed, dusted and vacuumed. She finally flopped in the lounge chair and surveyed her work. She had to admit it was a much needed improvement.

After a shower, Stacey spent the rest of the afternoon working on her hair, her nails and her face.

About five, Becky called. "Are you still here? When I didn't hear from you yesterday, I thought maybe you'd gone with your dad."

"Dad couldn't take me. I guess I'm stuck in town for the summer."

"I'm sorry things didn't work out for you, but I'm glad you'll be here. Would you like to go with me to the young adult meeting tomorrow night? An all-male ensemble from a big church in California is going to sing."

About to say no, Stacey thought of the empty hours she faced tonight and possibly tomorrow night, too. "Sure, why not?" she said. "Do you want me to pick you up?"

"No. I'm taking Dondra and one of her friends. I'll come by for you."

The next evening, Stacey left her room dressed in white: skirt, blouse and sandals. The only color was a vivid red belt exactly the shade of her nail polish and lipstick. A sparkling white sweater lay over her arm.

"You're going out?" her mother asked.

"Yeah. Becky's picking me up for some meeting at the church." Stacey saw a glimmer of hope in her mother's eyes.

"That's nice," her mother said. "Have a good time. I'm

working the late split shift again, so I won't be here when you get home."

"There's Becky. I have to go." Stacey ran out, letting the screen door bang behind her.

Dondra and her friend, Mira, were whispering in the back seat when Stacey slid in beside Becky. Though the two girls were only two years behind her in school, Stacey didn't know them well. She stiffened, wondering if the whispering and snickering were about her.

Becky smiled. "Hi. I'm glad you're coming with us. The program sounds great."

"Yeah," chimed in Dondra, "I hope the guys are handsome."

Stacey laughed, but squirmed inside. Coming from Dondra, the remark sounded childish, but it was the same idea she'd had. To cover her own thoughts, she said, "Guys from out of town always look better—until you get to know them. Then they turn out to be just like the guys you've always known."

Dondra and Mira vociferously denied her statement and told all they knew about the singers who were going to be at the meeting. They were still listing their merits when Becky pulled into the church parking lot.

Becky laughed. "I guess we get to see for ourselves now."

They piled out of the car and hurried in to find seats in the small auditorium. They'd just settled into place when Mike Havig bent over Becky.

"We need a piano player. JoLinda just called to say she can't be here."

Becky shook her head violently. "No. Mike, I can't play when a group talented enough to do a tour is here. Ask their accompanist to play for us, too."

Mike grinned. "I already did. They don't have one. They sing with taped music."

Becky groaned but smiled good-naturedly at the same

time. "Save my place, Stacey. I'll come sit with you as soon as I can."

Stacey felt conspicuous sitting alone. Though she'd come to these functions several times with Becky, she hadn't gotten well acquainted. She wished she could make friends as easily as Becky seemed to—and Erica.

Erica, who had started coming after she did, was already a central figure, with several of the kids grouped around her chatting. Was it because she was dating Mike, the leader? Or was it something in Erica herself?

The room filled, and the program started. After some lively Bible choruses, Mike introduced the leader of the ensemble. Becky slid into the pew beside her. Stacey felt better. She smiled at Becky and whispered, "You did fine."

The spokesman told a bit about the group and promised that each one would share a little about himself during the concert. "But first, we'll do what we do best—sing."

The twelve young men took their places, grouped around four separate microphones. Their music combined fun, rollicking tunes with more serious songs. And three or four of the group were really good looking.

Stacey got lost in a daydream where the bass singer asked her out. She imagined him really liking her and wanting to keep on dating for no reason other than that he enjoyed being with her. She felt an unaccustomed blush creep into her cheeks as his eyes met hers.

After three songs, the leader told what his life had been like before he came to know Jesus and the changes that had taken place since. Stacey divided her attention between wishing she were in Colorado with her father, dreaming about the handsome bass, and listening. She noted that a few things the man said meshed with what Becky had shared with her over the past few months.

After each group of selections, a different member of the ensemble gave a short testimony. The last was a tall, blond baritone with broad shoulders. "You know, my story is a lot like the others you've just heard, but, like them, I had my own personal struggles with coming to know Christ. Before He came into my life, I did something that I felt was okay at the time, but later I realized it was terrible."

Stacey straightened. That sounded like her. Could he have done something as bad as she had?

"A couple of years ago, my best friend was running for student body president. I had no desire for office myself, so I offered to be his campaign manager. Everything went well until he was chosen starting quarterback for the football team and I was left on the bench.

"That hurt. I'd always been considered the better athlete. Then insult was added to injury, as the saying goes. My girl didn't like dating a bench warmer, so she looked for more impressive dates." His strong face crinkled into a grin. "I didn't think it was funny then. I was angry and bitter."

He looked around the room, then his gaze seemed to linger on Stacey. "I decided my friend was the cause of all my problems, and I set out to get even. I thought he should discover what it was like to fail, to fall from the top to where rejection and mocking replaced near idolatry.

"So, I plotted and planned. As his campaign manager, I was in an ideal spot. While appearing to do all I could to get him elected, I sabotaged every plan. Then I really got a bright idea. I began starting rumors. It was easy. I'd just pick out a couple of people I knew loved to be the bearers of bad news and asked, 'Have you heard such and such about Davy?'

"It worked. Davy lost the election. I got my revenge, but the victory was hollow. Davy didn't seem to care. He said that the other guy would probably make a better student body president anyway. What was worse, he added, 'If God had really intended me to be president, I couldn't have lost.' "

The blond baritone shook his head as though he still couldn't believe that reaction. "I'd caused him to lose, and Davy was giving God all the credit."

A ripple of laughter interrupted.

"As the days went by, my schoolwork suffered because I felt so guilty about what I'd done. That's when my friend Davy finally got through to me about Jesus and His fantastic forgiveness. That's what I wanted most right then. So I leaned on the fender of Davy's old Chevy and silently told Jesus all I'd done—more than just the election thing.

"It was great. Jesus forgave me and I became a new person inside. But somehow, I still couldn't shake off the guilt. Finally Davy suggested that I might need to ask forgiveness from someone else. Was there anyone I felt I'd wronged that I needed to apologize to? I rebelled. It was the last thing I wanted to do. Confess to Davy, my best friend? Tell him what a rat I'd been?"

His face revealed the horror he'd felt at the thought. "But it wasn't long before I decided confession would be a lot easier than carrying around my load of guilt. Besides, if I didn't do something soon, my grades would be so bad I'd be cut from the team altogether and maybe not graduate.

"So, I told Davy. I confessed it all.

"And, you know what? He forgave me. A tremendous weight toppled off my shoulders. And I owe it all to Jesus, who first forgave me himself, then nudged me until I faced up to my guilt. He gave Davy the freedom to forgive me, too.

"If there's something bothering you tonight, if your guilt load is heavy, take it from me. It's far easier and a whole lot better to take it to Jesus. Let Him forgive. He promises to, you know. Then go on from there, living a new life in Him."

He stepped back to his microphone, and the ensemble sang one last song, then turned the meeting back to Mike. As he stood to close, Becky left to play for the closing song. Stacey sat very still. She felt as if her guilt flashed like a neon sign for everyone to see. She knew if she looked up, Erica would be glaring at her with blame and anger in her eyes.

When it was finally over, she stood next to Becky waiting to leave. She talked to a few people, but couldn't concentrate on anything anyone said.

Dondra and Mira came up, and Dondra pleaded, "Becky, most of the group are going to the Shanty for pizza. We'll go too, won't we?"

Stacey's heart dropped. She couldn't stand an hour or two with all these kids talking and laughing. She sighed in relief when Becky answered.

"I'm sorry, Dondra. I promised Mom I'd be home right after the meeting to sit with Dad for a while."

"Can we go, if we can get a ride?"

"Depending on the ride."

"Wait just a couple of minutes. We'll find someone."

Stacey edged her way out the door into the cool Puget Sound night. The fresh air felt good on her flushed cheeks. She walked toward Becky's car, drawing in several deep breaths, trying to calm her tumultuous thoughts.

Leaning against the car, she saw Dondra and Mira erupt from the building with Mike and Erica. Becky was right behind them.

"Thanks, Mike," Becky was saying. "I wish I could join you all, but I promised Mom." She laid her hand on Dondra's shoulder. "Remember, home by midnight."

"Sure. We'll probably be there before that."

Stacey stayed in the shadows by the car until the four had climbed into Mike's car and left. She called to Becky, "I'm over here."

"Everything all right?" Becky asked as she walked up.

"Yes. I guess I'm just tired." She thought about talking to Becky again about her guilt, but she knew what Becky would say.

Becky respected her silence while they drove. When they drew up in front of Stacey's house, Becky reached over and touched Stacey's hand. "I'm glad you came tonight, but you seem troubled. Anything I can do?"

"Not tonight. I'll be okay."

"We're starting a new Bible study next Thursday. Would you join us?"

"I don't know. Maybe."

"See you Sunday?"

"Probably. I'll let you know."

Inside, Stacey wandered around the empty house. She opened the refrigerator door, then decided she wasn't hungry. Restless, she went upstairs to get ready for bed. As she started to drop her clothes on the floor, she looked around the clean room. Hoping to start a new habit, she hung up the skirt, dropping the blouse into a hamper in her closet.

She wrapped her scarlet robe around her and when she started to cleanse her face. The phone rang.

Stacey ran out into the hall to answer. A melodious deep bass voice asked, "Is Mr. White in?"

"No. He's in Colorado."

"Oh. I thought I saw him a couple of days ago."

"He was here, but he's returned to the site."

"Could you tell me how I can get in touch with him?"

Stacey gave him her father's local office phone number. "You can reach him there tomorrow."

"It's rather urgent that I contact him tonight."

"I'm sorry. You can try that number, but I doubt anyone is there."

"Surely there's a way you can call him directly?"

This guy is too persistent, thought Stacey. She remembered her father's injunction over the years. "When I'm away on a project, give no information to anyone. If someone won't take no for an answer, get his name."

"Could I have your name? Perhaps tomorrow I can have him get in touch with you."

"Oh, he wouldn't recognize my name. But I know he'd want to talk to me. How about giving me your private number for him?"

Stacey thought she heard voices in the background behind her caller. She strained to make out what they were saying, but couldn't. "Sorry," she responded. "There is no private number. Contact his office in the morning."

She hung up before he could say any more.

Chapter Three

Stacey sighed. Too bad a man with such a nice voice wasn't calling her instead of being such a pest. A fleeting smile danced across her face. He was probably fifty, bald and fat. Pushing him from her mind, she finished her cleansing routine.

She forced herself to concentrate on the small chores of getting ready for bed; but when she finally curled under the light blanket, she could no longer shut out the thoughts of tonight's last speaker.

He'd made forgiveness sound so simple and so inviting. He'd talked about peace and freedom from guilt. How she longed for that.

She shifted restlessly. It would be heaven not to feel so wretched around Erica, to really be Becky's best friend, maybe even to become an insider with the church group— to have lots of friends. Best of all, to like herself.

Yet Becky had told her more was required. She couldn't just ask for forgiveness and then selfishly go her own way. God freely forgives, but He expects something in return: obedience, submission, doing everything the Bible said was right.

Stacey twisted to her left side. Was getting rid of the guilt worth becoming a slave for the rest of her life? What about her own desires? Her plans? Her independence? Could she give all that up?

Remembering the moment when it seemed her guilt was visible to everyone, she flopped over on her stomach and pulled the pillow over her head. She couldn't breath, so she flipped to her right side. Pummeling her pillow, she crammed it under her head and closed her eyes.

The clock on the landing struck midnight. Still her thoughts churned on. A gallery of faces passed in front of her eyes. First was the singer/speaker. His face had been less—far less—than handsome, but his eyes were quiet and peaceful. Something about him was appealing, drawing her to that peace. Becky's face took his place. Stacey knew the burdens and problems Becky endured, but she was always happy, always peaceful.

Becky was followed by Todd Jones, the guy Stacey had been dating—the one who talked her into the mess with Erica, writing insulting notes, spreading rumors. Stacey shivered a bit remembering his handsome face. He'd seemed to like her and treated her as if she were special, until she'd refused to write any more notes. She remembered his eyes—seeking, yearning, wanting something more. No. He had nothing she needed.

Erica emerged as Todd faded. Her face showed peace and contentment until she turned to look at Stacey. Then her expression changed, somehow conveying pity and accusation at the same time. Stacey squirmed. She didn't want anyone's pity. Would that happen if she asked for forgiveness?

Stacey groaned and jerked upright in bed. She pulled her knees to her chest and wrapped her arms around them. Closing her eyes and dropping her chin on her knees, she prayed, "Oh, God. I don't know what to do. I can't make a decision. It's too hard. I don't want to be a goody-goody. I don't want to be a slave. I just want to be me, but a nice me."

Stacey sat there thinking until the clock chimed one. The

sound reminded her of one of her Aunt Jess's favorite sayings, "Time heals everything." Maybe if she just waited, this horrid feeling would go away, and everything would be all right again.

Stretching out on her back and closing her eyes, she finally slept—but fitfully, with weird dreams—until she heard her mother come in from work at four.

She lay quietly, hoping to doze, but once more troubled thoughts started chasing through her head, and sleep was gone. After her mother settled into her room, Stacey rose and pulled on jeans and a cotton turtleneck sweater. Maybe bird watching would make the time pass that would heal this mess. She grabbed her binoculars and bird book.

The next book from the shelf fell to the desk. She started to cram it back, but the supple, soft-covered book refused to fit into the double space. Angrily she stared at the small blue New Testament. Becky had given it to her months ago. She'd stuck it on the shelf and forgotten all about it.

She reached her hand out again to replace the Bible on the shelf, hesitated, and drew it back. Would she find answers in it as Becky promised? Hesitantly, almost fearfully, she turned it over in her hand. After a moment or two, she put it in her backpack.

After a stop in the kitchen to pack some food and write a note to her mother, Stacey let herself out of the house.

As she backed out of the drive, she was surprised to see a telephone repairman in coveralls coming from across the street. He dropped a long aluminum ladder and bent over it as if adjusting something. For a moment she thought he looked familiar, but then absently shook her head. She was sure she didn't know any telephone men.

A plain gray panel truck was parked across the way and another coverall-clad man perched at the top of the nearest telephone pole. She caught a glimpse of a round flat face with a twisted nose before he turned to continue his work.

At this awfully early hour it seemed strange for someone to be out repairing telephones. Maybe somebody had complained.

She drove past the first man kneeling over his ladder, feeling a bit piqued that he didn't look up. Most men gave her a second glance. She shrugged. At least she didn't have to be at work this early in the morning.

Stacey parked in the same place as the day before and walked into the woods. Remembering the noisy whistler, she passed the cutoff she'd taken before and went on to the next trail that branched off to the left.

She found another cedar tree to hide under, spread out her food for the birds, and crept in to wait. She pulled her bird book out of the backpack, and her New Testament came with it.

The thoughts she'd been holding at bay while she drove and walked crashed in on her. She picked up the small blue book and stared at it. Gingerly she opened it and riffled through the pages. In the back were lists of some sort. Many of the pages throughout the book had sections highlighted in yellow.

Stacey read a word here and there, then flipped to another page. She turned to the beginning, thinking she might read through it while she waited for the her "mini's" to appear. But the first page said, "Abraham was the father of . . . the father of . . . the father of" . . . Dull. Nothing for her there.

She thumbed through the book again until one subtitle almost jumped off the page, grabbing her attention. "Slaves to righteousness." There, that proved it. If she wanted forgiveness, she'd have to be a slave.

She read the verses, then twisted to sit up, her legs crossed Indian fashion. According to the verses in Romans 6, she was already a slave. Her only choice was which master to serve: sin or righteousness.

The results were plainly laid out. Slavery to sin led to death; slavery to righteousness led to holiness and eternal life. Stacey ran her hand through her smooth black hair. That was no choice really. Anyone would choose life.

She really longed for life, but how could she make the

change? Stacey tried to remember everything Becky had told her, but she'd been resisting so hard each time Becky talked that she'd blocked it from her mind. She'd have to search more in the book.

She drew in a sharp breath. It was like someone was guiding her hands as they flipped from page to page through the little book. Near the front was an article on leading a person to faith in Christ. Eagerly she read until she came to a suggested prayer. She wanted to stop and pray, but decided to read on to the end first. The next page and a half contained Bible verses to prove the points made in the article.

Some of them didn't mean much to Stacey, but others were like they'd been written just for her. One in John 5:24, said, "I tell you the truth, whoever hears my word and believes him who sent me has eternal life and will not be condemned; he has crossed over from death to life."

Stacey looked at the words, whispered them aloud, and longed to have them true in her life. If only she could escape condemnation and move from death to life. She'd feel free even if she were a slave.

Nearby a flock of birds fluttered and tsited. Stacey glanced up, reaching for her binoculars. But then her hand dropped to the book again. This was more important.

She came to Romans 6 where she'd discovered slaves. She skipped past that one and stopped to reread Second Corinthians 6:2, "I tell you, now is the time of God's favor, now is the day of salvation." So, today was the day. The Bible said so, and her soul longed for the peace that seemed to be almost within her grasp.

But she made herself finish, hoping to find another clue. She found it in First John 1:9, "If we confess our sins, he is faithful and just and will forgive us our sins and purify us from all unrighteousness."

Marking her place with her forefinger, Stacey closed the book. She rested her cheekbone against its spine. "Jesus," she whispered, "I confess my sin. I was terrible to Erica, saying and doing such awful things. I've been nasty to my mother; I know I hurt her all the time. I'm not even very nice to Becky or anyone else. Please forgive me, like you promised in this book. Make me your slave."

Tears spilled from her eyes as sobs shook her body, wiping out the restless resistance she'd battled through the night. In its place crept a new feeling, one she couldn't describe, but it was wonderful.

The sobs diminished until they were mere hiccups in her breathing. She was fumbling in her backpack for a tissue, when a deep voice said, "Here. Use mine."

An arm dropped around her shoulders and another extended a snowy handkerchief. For a moment she almost felt it was Jesus Himself who'd come to comfort her. Then she twisted to see who'd invaded her private spot.

The tall, blond photographer from the day before knelt behind her, holding her gently. His hold tightened as another wave of sobs engulfed her.

Stacey leaned back against his shoulder, her head bowed, weeping into his handkerchief.

He let her cry for a few moments, then asked, "Want to tell me about it?"

She jerked. How could she tell him that seeing him made her remember she had something else to ask forgiveness for? He'd never understand. Besides, he'd probably laugh at her, and she couldn't bear being laughed at right now.

She shook her head. "I'm okay. The storm is over." Grabbing her backpack, she stuffed the Testament and her bird book and binoculars into it and crawled out from under the tree. She felt his hand at her elbow as she stood.

"How—How'd you find me?" she asked.

"I was taking pictures down this path. I'd shot all the film I had and was leaving when I heard someone crying. Remembering a certain someone's penchant for hiding under cedar trees, I just scouted out the largest one in the area, and there you were."

"I didn't hear you."

"I learned my lesson yesterday. When that certain spiky

someone complained about noise . . ."

Stacey felt that snapping sensation inside, a moment when she knew she had an instant to either smile or yell. Perhaps because of the knowledge of how tear stained and unkempt she looked, perhaps because of years of habit, she chose anger.

"You had it coming," she snapped, jerking her arm from his grasp. "Anyone who tromps through the woods when he's trying to take wildlife pictures has to be stupid. A—A moron would know better."

"Hey, I'm sorry." He looked bewildered, as if he couldn't understand her attack.

Well, she didn't understand herself. She just knew she had to get out of there. "Thanks for your handkerchief," she grunted, thrusting it back at him and running down the path toward her car.

Driving home, Stacey decided two things. She'd avoid the woods for the rest of the summer, and when she got home, she'd crawl into bed, ask for forgiveness for her burst of anger, and sleep until noon.

But as she walked through the back door of the house, she heard angry voices. *What now?* she wondered, dropping her backpack onto the kitchen floor.

Chapter Four

Stacey hesitated just inside the kitchen door, listening to the raised voices from the living room. One sounded like the man who'd called the night before. "Please, Mrs. White," he was saying. "We need to reach your husband immediately. I know you can help us."

Stacey tiptoed through the hall and up the stairs. She splashed cold water on her face to erase the trace of tears. She added a touch of mascara, then changed into fresh jeans and an ice-pink cotton top. After combing her hair, putting every shining black strand in place, she ran down the stairs and into the living room.

Pausing just inside the door, she surveyed the scene. Her mother's light blue eyes were almost colorless with suppressed anger. The same emotion brought out flaming circles at her cheekbones. Her rigid posture told Stacey her mother was ready to lose control.

Stacey caught her breath as she took in the other three people in the room. The two men were the same ones who'd been at the airport. Seeing them in her own living room scared her. Something about the older, balding man's stare raised goose bumps on her arms.

The other man was as good-looking as she remembered, with curly brown hair and chocolatey eyes. And he was smiling. Tentatively she smiled back before studying the woman. Her hair was as black as Stacey's, only worn short. Something about her made Stacey wish she'd dressed up.

Conversation stopped when Stacey entered the room. The woman broke the rather long silence. "Is this your daughter?"

A deeper distress washed over her mother's expression. "Stacey! I didn't know you'd be home so soon."

"Something came up. I'll tell you later." Stacey walked over and perched on the arm of her mother's chair, one elbow resting on the back, her hand just touching her mother's shoulder. Her blue eyes met the peculiar amber ones of the other woman. "Yes, I'm her daughter, Stacey. And you?"

The woman shifted under the direct stare, but smiled. "I'm Neva Boyce, a physicist like your father. And this," she gestured toward the balding man, "is Arnold Tenley." Her hand waved in the other man's direction. "Charlie Place. Both are connected with the government."

Stacey thought she saw a flicker of amusement in Charlie Place's face, but it was gone before she could be sure.

Arnold, the older man, said, "We've been trying to convince your mother we need to reach your father immediately. She doesn't seem to trust us."

"Should she?" Stacey asked.

The man glared at her with his opaque eyes, sending a shiver of fear sliding down her spine. She refused to be intimidated and stared back.

Charlie laughed and said, "Let me explain. Neva, here, was working on a project with your father when he was called away to the work he's doing now."

Stacey felt her mother stiffen even more and, glancing down, noticed her whitened knuckles. She looked back at Charlie. "Yes?"

"She's run into a problem and needs his assistance. Although we're not scientists, Arnold and I have been assigned to Neva to get her project finished. So, we came along to help get in touch with your father."

"I'm sure Mother has given you the number to call and the address." She paused and looked from one to the other. "In fact, if I'm not mistaken, I gave you that information last night."

Stacey thought she saw an expression of irritation cross his face, but he smiled again. "Yes, you did. We tried the phone number this morning, but were told your father wouldn't be available until next week or the week after. We can't wait that long, so we came to see if you could help us contact him." His glance flattered her.

"I told them that's the only number we have, but they don't believe me," Mrs. White said. "They're sure we have a direct line to him."

Stacey laughed. "Ridiculous. I'm sure Mother told you this is only a temporary assignment." She turned to Neva Boyce. "Seattle has lots of physicists. Why don't you contact one of them for help?"

Again Stacey noticed irritation covered by a smile. *This group is trying to be nice and having a hard time of it,* she mused, *but they're better at hiding anger than Mom.*

With a smile firmly in place, Neva said, "I guess you'd have to be a scientist to understand."

"I'm on my way to being a scientist," Stacey informed them. "Try me."

Charlie exchanged a look with Neva. "The way Ms. Boyce explained it to me is that once you're into a complicated process it takes so much to bring someone new up to that point it's like doing it all over again. It would waste valuable time, which Neva doesn't have."

Neva nodded. "It could save weeks if I could talk to Mr. White for an hour or so." She leaned forward. "Please, tell us how I can contact him."

Mrs. White, calm now, stood. With the old firmness that Stacey remembered, she confronted the visitors. "We have given you that information. If you're unable to contact him immediately, there is nothing I can do."

Silently Stacey cheered, but her sense of victory faded

as she met Arnold's glare. It held a threat that again set fear licking through her veins.

"Open the door for them, Stacey," her mother ordered in the same tone.

Stacey led the way to the front door and stood there while they walked out. Anger jerked Neva step by step like a puppet, and Arnold muttered under his breath.

Only Charlie seemed unaffected by her mother's abruptness. He grinned at Stacey, and his hand briefly touched her shoulder as he passed. Stacey found herself smiling back, responding automatically to the pull of his attention. Then she was angry at herself as she closed the door leaning against it for a moment. Why did she always respond to a smile and touch? Was he really attracted to her? Or was he another Todd Jones—planning to use her?

"Stacey?"

She walked into the living room. Her mother was fussily removing imperceptible traces of their visitors' presence. "Thanks for your support. They just wouldn't accept that we didn't have a direct way to contact your father, and I was getting angry and frustrated."

"I could tell. Did you believe their reason?"

"No. I might have, but that man lied."

"When he said Neva Boyce had been working on a project with Dad?"

"Yes. How did you know?"

"You stiffened when he said it." Stacey curled into a chair across from the one her mother had slumped into. "Who was Dad working with?"

"Carl and Martin. Your father was rather bored with it—just a routine assignment, nothing special."

"Could he have offered to help Neva—sort of as a sideline?"

"He never mentioned it. If the project were as difficult and urgent as Ms. Boyce indicated, Doug would have been excited enough to talk about it. He didn't."

Mrs. White straightened her shoulders and stood. "How about some breakfast?"

"Sounds good. I'm hungry." Stacey followed her mother into the kitchen. She set the table and fixed toast while her mother poached eggs and heated leftover ham. "Dad told me his current project was top secret, but why was Neva Boyce told he was unavailable 'til next week?"

"That sort of bothers me. In fact, this whole episode worries me."

"Do you suppose we should call Dad and tell him?"

Mrs. White paused over a forkful of egg. "I hate to cause him any anxiety when he's in the middle of an important project." She sighed. "But, at the same time, I have a feeling those three should be reported."

"Why don't we call the office and tell Dad's supervisor? He'll know whether to pass the information along to Dad or not."

Relief eased the tired lines in her mother's face. "Thanks, dear. That's just what we'll do." She finished eating, then bustled around the kitchen putting things away, cleaning up. "Before I do, tell me about the phone call last night."

"I recognized his voice," Stacey said, after a quick glance to see if her mother was being nosy or if she felt the call was important. "He wouldn't give his name last night, just tried to cajole me into giving him our private number for Dad. I told him there wasn't one and to try the office. When he persisted, saying he needed it immediately, I just gave him the same number again and hung up."

Stacey waited while her mother made the call to her husband's supervisor. In brisk tones, Mrs. White told exactly what had happened: the phone call last night, the visit this morning, and all that had been said.

When she finished, she laid her hand on Stacey's arm. "Thank you, dear. You've been a great help. The supervisor thanked me but said not to worry. He'd get back to us with any information we need about those three." She leaned for a moment against the door jamb. "I think I'll see if I can get some sleep. How about you?"

"I'm too wide awake." Stacey tried to keep the resentment from her voice. Old, familiar questions hammered at her. Why could they get along so well when they were protecting Dad? Why couldn't they always have an open and caring relationship? She forced herself to say, "I have a few things I need downtown. I'll probably go shopping."

They walked upstairs together. "Okay," her mother agreed. "Will you be home for lunch?"

"I doubt it. I'll be here for dinner, though."

Stacey took time to put away the things she'd dropped on the bed when she came in from bird watching. It would be a while before the stores opened anyway. She handled the little New Testament gently, starting to put it back on the shelf. Changing her mind, she tucked it in her handbag. Maybe she'd read more later.

Stacey showered and changed into white shorts and a scoop-necked tee shirt. She slipped into a pair of strappy white thongs, checked her mirror once more, grabbed up her clutch bag, and ran downstairs.

Striding briskly, her thoughts skipped over the visitors and their problems, back to the morning and her decision to ask God's forgiveness.

Would things really be different? she wondered. She didn't feel any different. Well, in a way, she did. A certain unhappiness was gone. Would it last?

After buying some red nail polish at the drug store, Stacey went next door to Penney's and selected a raspberry-colored terry short outfit.

Across the street was the Open Door, a Christian book store. Slowly she walked over and entered, with the vague feeling that she needed something to help her learn more about God. Maybe she would find it here. She wandered between the book racks, looking at titles. She picked up and paged through several books, but put them back on the shelves.

When the clerk finished with another customer, she asked, "Something I can help you with today?"

Stacey shook her head. She couldn't admit she didn't know what she wanted. With a faint sense of disappointment, she left.

After a few more stops, she wandered into the Bakery Cafe for lunch. The small restaurant had only a half dozen tables, all of them occupied. Stacey started toward one of the stools at the counter when she heard her name.

Turning, her heart seemed to stop, then thudded slowly on. Erica beckoned her with a smile. Too late to pretend she was waiting for someone, reluctantly Stacey walked the few steps to the tiny table for two crushed up against the wall.

"Join me for lunch," Erica invited, brushing brown hair back from her forehead. "I've just ordered."

Stacey sank into the empty chair. "Thanks. I just stopped for a quick burger. How's your summer?"

"Busy. Dad's given me the chance to be a full-fledged reporter. I've been trying to dig up newsworthy stories. It's harder than I thought, but fun. Are you working?"

"Not yet. I counted on working with Dad in the lab, but he's been assigned to a special project in Colorado and he couldn't wangle a place for me." Stacey was glad when the waitress stopped to get her order. She felt distinctly uncomfortable with Erica.

"How disappointing," Erica remarked, going back to their conversation when the waitress left. "What kind of lab does your father work in?"

"He's a physicist. He specializes in atomic structure and nuclear phenomena." For a moment she forgot her discomfort and talked eagerly. "It's an exciting field. I want to get into it myself, but I'm not sure what specialty appeals most. They're all so interesting, it'll be hard to choose."

"That means you'll be going to college this fall. Where?"

"Here at the U. At least for the first four years. I don't know beyond that."

By the time the waitress returned with their food, Stacey started to feel ill at ease again. The animation died from her voice. Stacey felt worse and worse with each bite. Finally she blurted, "How does your mother like her job by now?"

She could have bitten out her tongue. Why bring up that subject? She'd said some pretty nasty things about Erica's mother not too many weeks ago.

Erica didn't seem to notice. "She loves the job. But I think she's getting tired of being away from home. I heard her telling Dad the last time she was here that she's hoping to arrange a move back here before the full year in Boston is up." She sighed. "I sure hope so; it's not the same without her."

"I think I know. It's like when Dad is gone on a job for a long time. Like now." Stacey tried to suppress something inside which urged, *Ask for forgiveness. Do it now and get it over with. You'll feel better.*

She glanced at the other tables. They were so close that several were involved in one general conversation. If she apologized now, they'd all hear.

Does it matter? asked the prompting inside. *Wouldn't it feel good to be forgiven by Erica?*

But what if she won't forgive?

She will. The prompting voice continued, *I'll take care of the consequences. You do your part.*

"Is something wrong?" Erica asked. "You look troubled."

"Yes. Awfully wrong." She drew a deep breath.

Before she could go on, Erica reached out and grasped her hand.

Stacey looked down at the hand on hers, then up into Erica's brown eyes. Her voice came out in almost a whisper. "I need your forgiveness. I did something terrible to you."

She went on in a rush before Erica could respond. "I was the one who left those notes on your locker at school. I was paid to do it, but I wanted to, too. I wanted to hurt you because you had everything. But now I'm sorry I did it. Will you forgive me?"

"Of course." Erica squeezed her hand. "I won't deny those notes hurt at the time, but Tyson is the real culprit and he's being taken care of. It turned out for the best. I gladly forgive you."

Stacey released her hand and wiped away a tear that hung on her lashes, being careful not to smear her mascara. "Thanks." She tucked a strand of hair behind her ear and reached out to Erica. "Friends?"

"Friends." Erica's hand met hers in a warm clasp. They smiled at each other as the waitress stopped to ask if they wanted dessert.

"Let's splurge and celebrate," suggested Erica. "How about a fresh strawberry tart?"

"Sounds great. A cup of coffee, too." With new freedom born of a clear conscience, Stacey chatted with her former enemy, getting to know her.

Erica glanced at her watch and jumped up. "I've got to run. I have an interview in fifteen minutes. I don't want to be late. Are you coming to the Bible study next Thursday?"

"Probably. Becky mentioned it. See you there."

Erica stood. "Oh, I'm having a few of the kids over for snacks and games after church Sunday night. That's why I called you over in the first place. Would you like to come?"

"Thanks. I'd like that." She watched as Erica paid her bill and hurried out of the cafe. She had misjudged Erica. She really was nice when you got to know her. And better yet was how good it felt to get rid of her guilt. Stacey felt a great burden lift.

After paying for her lunch, she finished her shopping. She considered stopping by to see Becky, but decided to go home and read some more in the New Testament.

Stretched out on the chaise lounge in the sun, Stacey went back to the passages she'd read that morning. They were still as challenging as they'd been before. She began leafing through the small book, reading a bit here and there, delighted when she found one of the familiar verses.

Later that evening as Stacey finished cleaning up the kitchen, the phone rang. She heard her mother get up to answer. She smiled to herself when she remembered the astonished look on her mother's face when she'd offered to wash the dishes. The smile faded when she remembered the tired lines that had prompted her offer. Maybe there was more for which she needed to be forgiven.

"Stacey, the phone's for you."

Hastily Stacey wiped her hands and picked up the kitchen phone. The deep voice which responded sent a tingle along her nerve ends. Charlie Place. She knew before he told her.

"Are you busy Sunday evening?" he asked.

"Still trying to discover if I can reach my father faster than you?" Stacey couldn't help the cynicism.

"No. I promise we won't mention your father—at least his whereabouts or his work. I'd just like to take you to dinner."

She thought of her agreement to go to Erica's and shrugged. Erica wouldn't care. She'd understand. Besides, she wanted to know if this was another Todd Jones, just out to use her, or if the good-looking government man was really interested in her.

"Are you still there?" he prodded.

"Yes. Just thinking about my plans. I'm free for Sunday."

"I thought we'd try Indian cuisine. Okay with you?"

Stacey caught her breath. "Sounds great."

She hung up and turned to her mother, a small smile of triumph curving her lips. "That was Charlie Place, the guy who was here this morning."

"What did he want?"

"To take me to dinner. We're going out in style Sunday evening."

"Oh, Stacey . . . why? I'm sure he isn't someone that

you should get mixed up with right now."

Stacey froze inside at her mother's tone. "Maybe he's just whom I should get mixed up with. Who knows, maybe I can find out why he's so insistent on finding Dad."

"Why can't you let Doug's office take care of that? They said they would."

"But I'd miss an Indian dinner at that posh place in Bellevue. Anyway, I'm going." Her voice softened slightly. "It'll be okay, Mother. Nothing will happen."

Chapter Five

Stacey woke up Sunday morning feeling that something good was about to happen.

In those first half-conscious moments she only recognized a pleasant anticipation, then coming fully awake, she remembered today was her first day of going to church as a real believer. Would it be different?

Then there would be dinner with Charlie tonight. A faint cloud dimmed her feeling of euphoria. Would he like her for herself or was she just part of his job as she'd been to Todd Jones?

She shrugged and slid out of bed. Skirting the clothes that were once again beginning to pile up on her floor, she searched for her New Testament in the accumulation that had gathered on her desk. She had time to read before getting ready for church.

Back in bed, she propped pillows behind her and opened the New Testament. Riffling through pages until she came to what looked like a good starting place called Acts, she soon became fascinated with the story of Jesus' ascension into heaven.

A growl from her stomach reminded her it was time to get ready for the day. In fact, if she didn't get with it, she'd miss the nine o'clock service which most of the kids attended.

She tossed back the covers and ran for the shower. A few minutes later, fresh from a quick rub down, she checked through her closet. She wanted to look extra special for church, so several outfits ended up hanging over chairs and the bed before she found one that seemed to fit the occasion. The dress was bone-white silk with a softly draped neckline. It clung to her slender waist and fell in soft folds around her legs.

Stacey tucked the New Testament into a blue leather clutch bag and slipped her feet into matching pumps. Her mirror told her she couldn't look better. But for a moment a frown marred her face. Todd Jones had given her this outfit. Was it the right thing to wear to church? She shrugged. They were just clothes. It couldn't matter where she got them.

She had just finished a piece of toast when Becky drove up. She jotted a hasty note, "Mom, went to church with Becky. Be back before noon." She left it in the middle of the kitchen table, grabbed up her clutch bag and dashed out.

Stacey felt as if she'd burst if she didn't tell Becky about the decision she'd made in the woods Friday morning. And yet, something held her back, keeping her from breaking into Becky's chatter. Then they pulled into the church parking lot, and there wasn't time.

A little of the sparkle disappeared from the day. It almost seemed that Becky should have noticed a difference.

Stacey's disappointment was forgotten when the service started. Joining in the praise songs, she could sense a change in herself. Before, they'd just been catchy tunes that were fun to sing. Today her heart responded to the words, and they took on new and deeper meanings.

When the pastor introduced a new series of sermons based on Philippians, Stacey remembered seeing that name in her New Testament. She pulled it out of her bag and searched through its pages until she found the place.

Almost without conscious thought, she reached forward to take the sermon note paper provided in each pew. Eagerly she listened, jotting points and principles. She completely forgot Becky sitting beside her and her earlier idea to do something that would make Becky notice a change.

When the sermon ended and the invitation was extended, Stacey marveled that instead of her former uncomfortable, squirmy feeling, she yearned to respond, sensing that stepping out would fulfill her need to belong.

Hesitating, she glanced to either side at the number of people she'd have to pass. Becky's widened, surprised eyes met hers, questioning her. Stacey nodded, and Becky pressed back to let her ease her way to the aisle.

Stacey hardly noticed the crowd as she made her way forward. The pastor's smile and kindly eyes drew her and supported her. Then he shook her hand and with a warm pat on the shoulder, guided her to a counselor who stood waiting.

With the counselor, Stacey confirmed the decision she'd made in the woods and learned the importance of following that decision with baptism and involvement in a local church. She refused an opportunity to be baptized immediately, for an idea was growing in her mind.

"Does one have to be baptized in a church service?" she asked.

"No, not necessarily. What did you have in mind?"

"Well, Becky James has been praying for me and talking to me for months . . . years. Would it be all right if she did it? With maybe just a few other friends there?"

"I don't know. Do you want me to find out for you?"

"Would you please?"

The woman made a note on the personal information card Stacey had filled out at the beginning of the interview and promised, "I'll contact you within a day or two with an answer."

Stacey thanked her and hurried out, knowing she'd made Becky late. To her surprise, all the kids were waiting for her. First Becky, then Erica hugged her, and the others clustered around, hugging, shaking hands, patting her back, exclaiming and praising God.

Her initial reserve melted at the good will expressed, and she welcomed their genuine love and delight. Her eyes sparkled as she returned hugs and accepted good wishes. The acceptance she'd felt into God's kingdom deepened as one by one they told her how glad they were she had decided for Christ.

Becky touched her shoulder. "I hate to rush you, but I need to get home so Mom can come to the next service."

"Of course. I'm ready." With a smile and a friendly wave, Stacey followed Becky to the car. A warm glow filled her heart.

In the car, Becky demanded, "When did you accept Jesus, and why didn't you tell me?"

"Early Friday morning out in the woods. I don't know why I didn't tell you." Stacey glanced over at Becky. "I guess I wanted you to notice a difference. I had no idea I'd be going forward this morning."

"I'm so glad for you." Becky pulled up in front of the White home. "If you'd like me to show you some of the things a new Christian needs to know, I'd be glad to help."

Stacey paused with the door open. "Like what?"

"Oh, daily time spent with the Lord, memorizing verses, giving, obedience, helping. There're lots of disciplines we all should learn and practice in order to grow and to honor God."

"I guess the fact that I don't even know what needs to be learned shows I need some help. When do we start?"

"How about four this afternoon? Then we can stop for pizza or something and go on to church."

Stacey winced. "I can't go to church tonight. I have a date. But let's meet at four. Do you want me to come to your place?"

"If it's all right with you, I'll come to yours. We'll have fewer interruptions."

"Sure. Sounds great, see you at four."

Stacey hurried into the house. "Mom, I'm home," she called.

"Oh, Stacey. I'm so glad. Come into the kitchen. I'm fixing brunch."

"I'll run up and change clothes first. Be right there." Stacey ran lightly up the stairs. Perhaps things would improve between her and her mother now. She tossed her clothes aside and slipped into jeans and a tee shirt.

Determined to build a better relationship with her mother, Stacey entered the kitchen saying, "Umm, smells good. Fresh cinnamon rolls."

Her voice dragged to a halt as her mother turned from the sink. Tendrils of graying hair had escaped their neat French roll and clung to a face lined with anxiety. "Mom, what's wrong?"

"I'm worried. I tried to contact Dad today and couldn't get him."

"But, Mom, he's probably just engrossed in lab work."

"No. It's not that." Mrs. White put fresh rolls, scrambled eggs, and bacon onto the table. She poured orange juice, then motioned Stacey to sit down and eat. "I talked to the head of the lab here, then I called the office number and talked to someone in Colorado."

"And?"

Mrs. White's fingers shredded a cinnamon roll. "Both assured me everything was fine. The man in Colorado said they were checking up on the people who were here Friday morning, but had nothing to report yet."

"That sounds normal. What worried you?"

"The fact that I can't get in touch with Doug himself."

Stacey put her fork down and rested her chin on her hand. "But, Mom, if he's in the lab, he can't just walk out in the middle of an experiment or project."

"Of course not. But if he were in the lab, they'd say so. They didn't. All they'd tell me was that he was unavailable to come to the phone, that everything was all right, and he'd call as soon as he could."

Something of her mother's concern transferred itself to Stacey. Still she sought for a way to lessen her mother's worry. "Uh, you know this project is top secret. Maybe he's in conference with some high government official they can't talk about. That might explain their generalities."

Her mother's fingers stilled, and hope lightened her face. "Maybe. That could explain it." She nibbled at some of the torn pieces of roll. "I'll not feel right about it until I hear from Doug. I don't like having strangers almost force themselves into my home. They frightened me."

"But they can't have anything to do with Dad's being unavailable. They can't find him either."

"That may be, but I didn't like them. That older man's eyes were like knives, cutting right through me, and the woman's—never have I seen such coldness in a woman's eyes. It was like she wasn't human."

"I agree about the bald guy." Stacey shivered just remembering. "His look sent goose bumps dancing up my back."

"The other one wasn't much better. He was just like—"

"Like who?"

"No one. Forget I said it." Mrs. White jumped up from the table and busied herself clearing and tidying. She paused in her work to glance at Stacey. "Thanks for making me feel better. I hope you're right."

"I'm sure it's something simple," Stacey replied. "Dad'll call pretty soon, and we'll realize how foolish we are for fretting."

Her mother nodded, and the frown returned. "I—I," she pressed her lips together, then words burst out as if she could contain them no longer. "I wish you weren't going out with one of them tonight. I'm worried about that, too."

"Don't be, Mom. Maybe I'll find out something. Besides, I can take care of myself."

"He's much too old for you."

"Oh, Mom. It's not like I'm planning to marry him or something. I'm just going out to dinner. What can happen?"

"You'd be . . . oh, well. I can't convince you anyway. What are you doing this afternoon?"

"Becky is coming over for a while. Are you working today?"

"No. I think I'll see if I can sleep." Mrs. White paused at the kitchen door and looked long at Stacey. "If I don't see you before your date, do be careful."

"Of course, Mother."

Stacey poured herself another cup of coffee and sat at the table to drink it. She thought over the conversation with her mother. It had gone better than usual, but she felt ambiguous—glad she'd gotten her way, but resentful that her mother hadn't been firmer. Would other mothers let their daughters do exactly what they wanted?

She had to face the answer honestly. Most would, especially when the daughter was eighteen and stubborn. Maybe her mother gave in just to avoid arguments. Maybe her mother wasn't the one to blame.

She was still wondering about it hours later when Becky arrived. Pushing the thoughts away, she welcomed her friend.

Becky carried her Bible, a notebook and a couple of other books. "I'm ready if you are."

"I guess I'm ready. What do I need?"

"Nothing, really. Where are we going to work?"

"How about here in the living room?"

"Okay." Becky plopped her books on the coffee table and made herself comfortable on the sofa.

Stacey had just curled up in an adjacent chair when her mother came downstairs. "Hi, Becky. How are you?"

"Fine, Mrs. White. Isn't it great news about Stacey?"

Mrs. White's eyebrows lifted in question.

"About her accepting Christ. We're all so glad."

"Oh, yes . . . yes. It is nice." She looked at Stacey with a faintly puzzled frown.

Stacey stared down at her hands. Her mother wouldn't understand, and it would be one more conflict between them.

"Come on, Becky. We'll go up to my room, then Mom can be comfortable here."

"Don't rush off because of me. I'm just going to watch a tape on TV."

"We're going to be studying—sort of," Stacey explained. "My room is better."

But when they entered her cluttered room, Stacey wished she'd cleaned it up. The look on Becky's face was almost like that on her dad's when he'd seen it.

Quickly Stacey scooped up her clothes and dumped them in the closet, promising herself she'd hang them up as soon as Becky left. "I had a hard time deciding what to wear this morning," she said, trying to excuse the mess.

"It's easy to leave things in a shambles," Becky agreed while she settled into the arm chair Stacey cleaned off for her.

Becky glanced around the room. "This looks like military spit-and-polish clean compared to what my room used to be. I began to realize that, with Jesus living in me, He was there in my room and had to put up with the mess with Dondra and me. Since He's an orderly God, I knew it didn't please Him any more than it did Dondra, who's compulsively neat. Pretty soon, I couldn't stand the mess either and had to get it cleaned up."

"I kind of understand. Last Tuesday when Dad was here, he was pretty taken back by the mess. He said he couldn't understand how someone who groomed herself as I did could emerge from chaos like this."

"Exactly. God wants us to learn to do some things that may have no effect on eternal issues, but which help us grow to be the person He designed us to be." She grinned. "I can still hear my Grandma nagging me, telling me that cleanliness is next to godliness. I always meant to see if that was in the Bible, but I never have."

Stacey scribbled on a pad against her knee. "Okay. Practice neatness and keep my room clean. What else?"

"Most important is to spend some time each day talking to God."

"You mean praying?"

"Yes, but also letting Him talk to you through the Bible."

"I did that this morning. I read the first couple of chapters in Acts. Is that what you mean?"

"Yes. It works best for me to choose a book like Acts, Proverbs or Colossians, then read through it, making notes on things that seem important."

"How much do you read?"

"It depends. Some days, it may be a couple of chapters, others only a verse or two. I don't try to read any specific amount. I read until something sparks a response that I can think about through the day."

Stacey held up the New Testament Becky had given her. "This is all I have. I went to the Christian book store the other day, but there were so many Bibles I didn't know which one to get."

"The New Testament is enough to start with, though you'll eventually want a whole Bible. When you do, get one that is written in today's language—like that New Testament. They're so much easier to understand."

Stacey scribbled for a minute on her pad, then asked, "What next?"

"That's probably enough for your first week. Oh, one other interesting thing, though. Dad told me that because Bible people named their children according to characteristics that were desirable, he and Mom chose our names because of their meanings. Then they tried to raise us so that we'd live up to them. For instance, my name means 'captivator.' " She chuckled. "He did admit that I captivated their hearts immediately, but their idea was that I'd also captivate hearts for Jesus."

"That's neat. I was named after both my grandmothers."

Becky waggled one of the books she'd brought. "I've looked up both your names in this name book. Carolyn means 'one who is strong.' You could strive to be strong in Christ."

"What does Stacey mean? Since that's my first name and the one I'm going by now, that's the most important to me." Stacey slid off the bed to watch over Becky's shoulder as she found the place.

"It means 'one who will rise again.' Hey, that's great. That's God's promise for everyone who becomes a Christian."

A wistful look shadowed Stacey's eyes as she settled back on the bed. "I like that—better than being strong. I tried to be strong in my old life and made a mess of things. I could make the same mistake about strength again, but I can't rise again without God. I'm glad my new name matches my new life." She confided in Becky, "Dad has almost always called me Stacey, but Mom struggles with it. Do you think everyone else is having a hard time adjusting?"

"It was hard at first—sometimes we still forget, but if you remind us, we'll do better."

They talked for a while longer, and Becky gave Stacey a booklet to read and study about her new Christian life. "We'll get together next Sunday afternoon to discuss it, okay?"

"Sure . . . and thanks, Becky. Without you, I probably wouldn't be a Christian today. You did captivate me, though at times I wished you'd talk about something besides Jesus. Thanks for being persistent and for loving me even when I wasn't very lovable."

Becky moved to sit beside Stacey and hugged her warmly. "Thank you," she murmured. "Someday soon, you'll be used by God to bring someone to Him, and you'll know how very special and wonderful I feel right now." She brushed tears from her lashes and jumped up. "If I don't get moving, I'll be late for church."

"What time is it? Oh, I'll never be ready for my date on time."

They hurried downstairs together. At the door, Stacey gave Becky a hug. "Thanks again. Oh," she hesitated. "Are you going to Erica's tonight?"

"Yes."

"Would you tell her I can't be there? I told her I'd go before Charlie asked me out." Stacey noticed a frown cross Becky's face. "Is there something wrong with dating Charlie?"

"Not that I can think of. But we'll talk about it when we have more time. Bye."

Stacey dashed back upstairs, showered and began rummaging through her clothes for just the right thing to wear. The clothes she'd tossed in the closet earlier were once again strewn over the bed and chairs.

She finally chose a forest green two-piece dress she'd only worn a couple of times. With care, but speed, she applied mascara and green eye shadow. She finished her makeup and closed the door on her mess, starting down the stairs just as the doorbell rang.

"I'll get it," Stacey called to her mother, who lingered just inside the kitchen.

She opened the door for Charlie. As his eyes widened with admiration, she felt that perhaps he *was* interested in her for herself, not for what information he could get from her.

She turned to pick up a light summer coat and automatically checked her appearance in the mirror. She caught a look on Charlie's reflected face that belied his earlier admiration. His good looks were somehow transformed into the appearance of a vulture about to attack.

A shiver of disappointment and apprehension ran through her, but when she turned toward him, he smiled down at her and asked, "Ready?"

She nodded. "Ready."

Chapter Six

Charlie's hand cradled Stacey's elbow possessively as he walked her to the car and helped her into the passenger seat. He let his fingers slide down her arm and squeezed her fingers intimately before closing the door.

So that's the game we're playing, Stacey thought bitterly. And, she admitted to herself, she would have fallen for it again if she hadn't caught that glimpse of his face in the mirror. Well, two could play at the same game. She'd use him to find out all she could while keeping him from finding out anything.

When he slid under the wheel, Stacey smiled and turned in the seat to face him. It was a friendly posture which, at the same time, put her as far from him as possible. It also gave her the opportunity to watch him as he drove.

"You're beautiful tonight, Stacey." Charlie reached for and held her hand. "Now just relax. We're going to have fun, remember? I promised no probing about your father."

His warm touch made her realize how tightly she was grasping her clutch bag. She wriggled her shoulders and let her hands relax, lifting them from her lap and turning them palms up, letting go of his hand. She flexed her fingers and laughed. "Guess I'm a bit nervous being out with a government man."

"I'm no different than any of your other dates. Just a

guy who thinks you're attractive and interesting. Forget my job tonight."

Fat chance, Stacey thought. Aloud she said, "If I did that, how could I get to know you? Tell me, what do you do? Which branch of the government do you work for?

Stacey saw his eyes narrow and the corner of his mouth quirk as he answered. "We're loosely attached to the Office of Security."

"We?"

"Arnold Tenley and I."

"Oh. Why then would you be assigned to help Neva finish a project in physics? That doesn't compute."

"It does if her project affects the security of the nation."

"Does it?"

"Can you keep a secret?"

"Better than most." *Including you*, she mused.

His glance assessed her face, then swung back to the freeway. "I can't tell you much. Just that the project she's working on was commissioned by the Department of Defense and is highest priority. Speed is also essential. That's why we're trying so desperately to reach your father. He's the key to a breakthrough in one particular phase. Neva has his notes, but can't decipher one formula."

For a moment his attention was taken with moving into the exit lane and onto the off ramp. "But, there, you've made me break my promise. I didn't intend to talk business or to mention your father."

It all sounds so plausible, she thought. Could her mother be wrong? No. Dad would have at least mentioned such an interesting assignment even if he couldn't tell them anything about it.

"It seems to me that such a vital project wouldn't be assigned to just one physicist. I'd expect a whole phalanx of scientists to be concentrating on the project."

"Of course." Did his mouth tighten in irritation before he smiled? "About thirty of them, scattered around the country. A team like us is attached to each one."

"Why doesn't she just contact one or all of them? Certainly they're up on the project and don't need to spend weeks familiarizing themselves with the background."

"You don't miss a thing, do you?"

"It only makes sense. Why does she have to contact Dad? Why not one of the others currently working on the same project?"

"Don't ever let her know I told you this . . ." He paused and smiled. "Neva had a tough time landing the job. They didn't want a woman, and they didn't want someone with so little real experience. She fought hard to get this chance and feels she'll blow it if she yells for help."

"That's crazy. I'll bet every one of the others call for help all the time."

"Likely, but you can't convince Neva that she has the same right. She's determined to do it on her own or at least with help she scrounges up herself."

"If the project is as important as you say, she's letting pride and personal ambition interfere with the safety of our country. She doesn't deserve the job." Stacey caught her breath and forced herself to relax. She was reacting as if the story he was handing out were true.

Maybe it was just as well. She sensed him relax as he pulled through the porte cochere and stopped. Immediately a porter opened her door and helped her out while another opened Charlie's door and slid behind the wheel.

Charlie laughed as he joined her. "Spoken like a true patriot. Now, can we forget all this for the evening and just enjoy ourselves?"

Stacey smiled her agreement, making mental reservations about how relaxed she'd be. She'd stay alert for any questions that would elicit information she didn't intend to give.

The thought passed to the back of her mind, though, as they were ushered to their table. The softly lit dining room glowed with the shine of polished tables and sparkling crystal. Bright red napkins lent color while tree-size potted plants scattered throughout the room gave an outdoor feel.

As they studied the menu, Charlie explained some of the dishes and recommended his favorites. They chose to order a variety of dishes served family style.

True to his word, Charlie avoided all mention of Stacey's father and his work. The closest he came was in discussing the best universities for science majors. They also talked about sports and music.

Stacy enjoyed Murg Tikka, an Indian chicken entree baked in a clay oven; barbecued bread; and saffron flavored rice. She liked the quiet attention Charlie paid her, his courtesy and humor; but she soon realized that they had nothing in common. *Just as well*, she thought, *since this relationship will go no further than how much one can use the other*. A little splinter of ice pricked in her heart. Would anyone ever like her just for herself?

"I'm amazed at how light it stays so late," Charlie commented as they drove back to Karston.

"The longest day of the year is Saturday, and we're far enough north to get really long days."

"How about a walk before I take you home?"

"That would be nice. If you drive up to Blackman Lake, we can stroll along the shore."

"Just the thing. Will you be warm enough?"

"I think so. If not, we can always go back."

They meandered through the park and down toward the lake. Stacey was sure he'd at least hold her hand and try to soften her up, but he walked with his hands jammed into his pockets, kicking at the turf.

"I could almost imagine myself by a lake way out in the woods if those streetlights didn't interfere." He laughed. "It's been a long time since I visited the mountains or got much off the beaten track. I've forgotten how nice it could be."

"You've also forgotten how quiet a mountain lake and forest are. There's far too much traffic noise here to let the imagination transport one to the woods."

"Maybe. All the same, I'm enjoying it."

Stacey tucked a strand of hair behind her ear. "There is a place south of town where I like to go bird watching. It has its intruders, but by and large it's quiet. No ponds or lakes, though. Just stagnant pools here and there in the low places."

"Sounds like you enjoy quiet woodsy places. Is that the kind of vacation your family takes?"

"Sometimes." Stacey turned to retrace their steps. "We find it relaxing and yet full of all the activity we want."

"Is there someplace special you go?"

Stacey looked up. In the darkening night, she couldn't distinguish any expression in his face. Was he just talking or was he back to digging for information? She'd test a little.

"There's a cabin in the Cascades where we've spent a lot of time over the years."

"Oh?"

Was his voice too casual? She pretended to stumble and reached for his arm.

Quickly he steadied her, then drew her hand close and held it. "You were telling me about that cabin. Is it one of those resort places?"

Despite his seeming offhand interest, the muscles of his arm had tightened. So . . . now was the time for quick thinking. "No. Our own."

"Lucky you. Is it close enough to the ski resorts to use for skiing?"

He was definitely probing. Did he think her dad was hiding out there? Here's where she'd lead him on a wild goose chase. "The closest route was by cross country skis. Dad and I did that. But you can't really be interested in our family cabin. Tell me about your favorite vacation places."

She kept asking questions about his surfing in Hawaii and scuba diving in the Caribbean until they arrived back at her house.

"Thanks for a lovely evening," she said, opening the door. "The food was delicious."

"We'll do it again—soon."

"Perhaps. Good night and thanks again." She watched as he ran down the walk and drove off.

"Stacey?"

She went into the kitchen where her mother was having a snack before heading for work. "Mom, I really appreciate that you've been remembering to call me Stacey now. Why have you always called me Carolyn rather than Stacey?"

"It . . . it just happened. Why?"

After a moment's hesitation, Stacey said, "Remember what Becky said this afternoon? About my accepting Jesus? Well, I did. I've started a new life. I don't know enough to explain it yet, but Becky looked up the meanings of both Carolyn and Stacey. I decided I liked the meaning of Stacey better, so now I'm *really* glad I switched names. Besides, it seems to be Dad's favorite."

"After eighteen years of calling you Carolyn, it has been hard to switch, but I'm trying." Almost under her breath, she added, "It can't matter any more."

"What, Mom?"

"Nothing."

"Is there a reason why you never called me Stacey?"

For a moment Stacey thought her mother wouldn't answer, then slowly she said, "The person you were named for is someone who was extra special to your dad as a young man. She was like a second mother to him. I always resented that attachment, because she never approved of me as the right wife for Doug."

Stacey sat silently as her mother continued. "Even after all our years in a very satisfactory marriage, I couldn't forgive her for trying to keep us apart. I didn't want to name you Stacey, but I didn't want to hurt your dad either. Foolish, aren't I?"

Awkwardly, Stacey put her hand on her mother's shoulder. "No, you're not. I think I understand."

With unaccustomed tenderness, her mother reached to pull her close. "Thanks—Stacey."

The next evening they were just ready to sit down for dinner when the phone rang. Stacey jumped to answer. She signalled for her mother to pick up the phone in the den. "Hi, Dad."

Her mother ran for the other phone. "Doug. Are you all right?"

"Of course. Everything is okay. Our communication system broke down a little and it took some time to get in touch with me. Nothing to worry about."

"But we did worry. Where were you?"

"Closeted for some heavy concentration. What's this about Neva Boyce wanting me?"

"Do you know her?" Mrs. White asked.

"Not really. I've heard the name."

"Well, she says," Mrs. White's voice turned icy cold, "she's working on some project and needs you to help her with something that you worked on with her before you left."

"I what?"

"Worked on this project with her."

Stacey broke in. "In fact, Dad, it's supposed to be a top secret Defense Department project. Urgent, both in time and importance. Supposedly you left some notes with her, but she can't decipher one of the formulas."

"Where did you hear that?" both her parents asked simultaneously.

"You don't know anything about it?" Stacey asked.

"No. I've never even worked with anyone named Boyce, and I haven't heard of any urgent defense project either. I'd know if something like that were going on. Who told you?"

"I had a date with Charlie Place last night. That was his explanation for why they were in such a dither to find you."

"Charlie, who's Charlie?" her dad asked.

"Remember those two guys at the airport? They're the ones who were here with Neva Boyce. Charlie Place is the younger, good-looking one."

Her father was silent for what seemed like a long time.

"He's bad company to keep, Stacey."

"I know, Dad."

"What's going on, Doug? Something is wrong, isn't it?"

"No, dear," he comforted his wife. "Those two men are just a minor complication that has nothing to do with me—or us. I can't figure out why they're bothering you. But I think you can forget about them now."

"Dad, something else."

"Yes?"

"Charlie also quizzed me about our vacation cabin. I got the idea he might be trying to find out where you could be."

"Our vacation cabin? But we sold that years ago."

"I know, but I didn't tell him that. I only said it was within cross-country skiing distance from the ski resort."

Her dad laughed. "By the time we skied across that particular five miles to the slopes, we were so tired we couldn't make the first downhill run."

"I didn't tell him that, either."

Mrs. White joined in their laughter. "I guess that helps make up for their rudeness." She sobered. "Any instructions or advice for us, Doug?"

"Just keep on as you've been doing. Except, Stacey?"

"Yes?"

"If that Charlie comes around again, stay away from him. You may have bested him this time, but he's no one to fool around with. Okay?"

"I really doubt he'll be back, Dad. So don't worry."

"Take care of yourselves. I should be able to make it home for a weekend soon. I miss you both."

"Bye, Dad." Stacey hung up and busied herself re-warming their dinner while her mother and father finished talking.

Late Tuesday afternoon, Becky called. "How are things going?"

"Terrible. I've been job hunting with no results."

"Where've you looked?"

"Everywhere I could think of that is the least in the science line. Nobody wants to hire a high school graduate with no experience."

"Yeah. I know what you mean. Have you thought of trying something like a restaurant, the library, or selling in a department store?"

"Ugh. I doubt if I'd last an hour doing any of those things. But I may have to try. I don't want to just sit around for the summer."

"Are you coming to the new Bible study Thursday night?"

"Sure. Do you want me to pick you up?"

"No, I'll meet you there. I may be a little late. Dad's starting treatments again."

"I'm sorry. Is he a lot worse?"

"I don't think so. They just want to make sure." Becky paused a moment. "How are you doing with your Bible reading?"

"It's slow. Yesterday I forgot all about it. This morning I read some things that didn't make sense. Do you think that maybe I'm not really a Christian?"

"Stacey, remember we have a spiritual enemy who loves to sow seeds of doubt? Have you read that book I left?"

"Not yet."

"Try reading that tonight or in the morning. It'll answer those questions for you."

"Okay. I'll do it tonight."

"I'll be praying and I'll see you Thursday night. Oh, by the way, the study is on the Song of Solomon. It's a book in the Old Testament. You may want to be sure to have a whole Bible with you."

The next day, Stacey got home shortly after noon, hungry and discouraged. She'd been job hunting with no success.

When her mother met her at the door, Stacey could tell

something had happened. Her mother was obviously upset. "Carolyn, I'm so glad you've come."

"Stacey, Mom."

"Okay, okay." Her mother was ringing her hands and pacing around the front room. "I don't know what to do. If I should call . . ." Her voice faded out.

"What is it?"

"Come, look." Mrs. White led the way into the den. All the desk drawers were pulled out and papers strewn around. Several of the books were off the shelves. "My little recipe desk in the kitchen and your desk look the same."

"Is anything missing?"

"I can't tell. Who remembers what papers were in these desks?"

"Should we call the police?"

"I don't know. Do you suppose this has anything to do with Neva and top secret projects? No." Mrs. White answered her own question. "Why would they look for anything here?"

"Did you try to call Dad?"

"Yes. The line was busy."

"Let's try again." Stacey walked over and looked down at the ransacked desk. "What a mess." She picked up the receiver and dialed. "Still busy. I'll go check my desk and see what damage they did."

In her room, Stacey dropped her handbag and sweater on the bed. The desk was a worse mess than usual, but not nearly the disorder that marked her father's desk in the den. She leafed through things and put them back in drawers, certain that nothing had been taken.

After changing into jeans and a navy tee shirt, Stacey went back downstairs. "Have you gotten through?"

"No. I don't remember that line being busy for so long before."

"We never were quite so urgent before. Why don't we fix something to eat? It'll give us something to do until we reach them."

Stacey fixed sandwiches while her mother put out cut vegetables, relishes, and chips. They sat down, but neither felt very hungry. They managed to eat a little of what was in front of them, but finally Mrs. White said, "It's no use. I'm going to try again."

This time she got through. Stacey slipped into the den to listen.

"This is Mrs. White. Can I speak to Doug White right away?"

"I'm sorry. They're in the lab right now and can't be disturbed."

"Is Mr. Arthur there?"

"Just a moment."

"This is Arthur. Mrs. White? Something I can do?"

"I don't know. You know the trouble with those people who were here?"

"I remember."

"I'm not sure it's the same ones, but someone broke into the house this morning while we were gone and ransacked the desks."

"Take anything?"

"Not that I can determine. Stacey, did you find anything missing?"

"Nothing, Mom."

"When did you discover this?"

"About twelve-thirty."

"Have you reported it to the police?"

"Not yet. I thought you should know first."

"Good. I'll send a couple of men out to check. They'll be CIA. Check their ID carefully. Not that anyone would want to get in again while you're there, but I don't like this. Wish I knew what's going on."

"I wish it would stop. Is . . . Is Doug working on something dangerous?"

"No. Same kind of assignment as usual. Don't worry. We'll find out what's up and take care of it."

When they'd hung up, Stacey said, "I don't know if he comforted me or scared me."

"I know." Her mother wrung her hands. "He scared me. And there's lots he isn't telling us."

Chapter Seven

Stacey poured her mother another cup of coffee. "Come on, Mom, finish your sandwich."

"I can't eat."

"You need to relax. There's nothing we can do anyway. The CIA will take care of it. We don't have to do anything. That's what Mr. Arthur told us."

"But why the CIA? Why not just the local police? I don't understand what's going on."

Her mother's words sent prickles of fear dancing along Stacey's nerves. She ignored them, striving to remain calm. "We'll ask the CIA agents when they get here. There's probably some simple explanation—like the importance of the project Dad is working on. Maybe Boyce and her agents think he left information lying around here."

Mrs. White brushed tendrils of hair from her forehead. "Do you think that's all it is?"

"It sounds reasonable to me. Dad said he was working on a top secret project. Probably nothing more than any other that he's done over the past ten years, just that someone wants information on this one."

"I don't know why I'm so apprehensive about this. I almost dread finding out what will happen next."

"Maybe because nothing like this has touched us before. Having a stranger enter and rummage through our home is awful. It gives me the creeps. When we studied crime in our civics class this spring, they said most people feel vulnerable after a break-in, as if they've been violated."

Mrs. White jumped when the doorbell chimed.

"You *are* edgy, Mom. I'll get it."

Stacey hurried to answer. She peered through the viewer. Before her mother nudged her aside, she saw two men on the porch, both holding identification folders. Stacey unlocked the dead bolt, saying, "It's the CIA."

The taller of the two men presented his ID for closer scrutiny. "I'm special agent Mark Riley. This is special agent Richard Dicks. Mr. Arthur arranged for us to come and talk with you."

Special agent Dicks smiled, and his face lit up like a mischievous schoolboy's. "The calvary to the rescue, so to speak."

"I'm so glad you're here." Mrs. White examined the cards carefully, then handed them back. "Come and look."

She led the way into the den, then stood aside so the two agents could approach the desk.

"Have you touched anything since you found it this way?" asked agent Riley.

"I picked up some papers and put them down again." As if defending her action, she added, "Mr. Arthur asked if anything was missing and I started to check." Mrs. White's hands fluttered. "They're all Doug's things, and I wouldn't know if anything was missing or not."

Agent Riley nodded. "Richard, if you'll start fingerprinting, I'll just browse around." He took a small black object from his pocket and walked around the room. The thing fit snugly in his hand. He pressed a button with his thumb and the little black box seemed to come alive.

It made no noise, but vibrated—stronger and stronger as he approached the fireplace.

"What is—" Stacey began.

"Just routine fingerprinting," agent Riley broke in.

"While Richard is busy there, why don't you show me the other desks."

Stacey looked from one agent to the other. Both shook their heads, indicating silence. Before her mother could ask the question almost dropping from her lips, Stacey laid a hand on her arm. "Sure. Right this way. The next one is in the kitchen."

Agent Riley nodded approval and followed them. "What do you keep in the kitchen desk?"

As Stacey walked toward the kitchen, she watched the black matchboxlike thing in the agent's hand. It remained still. Had he turned it off?

Her mother, a bewildered look on her face, replied, "My cookbooks, recipes, menus." Her attention was on the box Riley held. "I keep household bills there, so receipts and things like that are in the desk."

"Wouldn't think anyone would be interested in disturbing that."

"As far as I can tell, everything is there that should be."

Agent Riley indicated the box in his hand. "We call this little item a 'sniffer.' It silently detects hidden electronic bugs. That way, if we decide we want to keep the bug in place, whoever planted it is unaware it's been found."

"You mean someone has been listening to everything we say in the den?" Mrs. White's voice shook.

"Probably not yet. They most likely left it this morning when they searched the desks."

"Are you going to leave it there?"

"For now. We'll have to report back and determine the best thing to do."

Stacey laid a comforting hand on her mother's arm. "We don't have to go in there, Mom. We don't spend much time there, anyway, when Dad's not home." She turned to the agent. "You will check out the rest of the house?"

"Of course. We also want to find out how they got in and any other clues they may have left behind."

When the agents had finished on the first floor, Stacey

and her mother led them upstairs. "I'm afraid I put every-thing back in my desk," Stacey confessed. "I didn't think about fingerprints." She breathed a sigh of relief that she'd also taken time to hang up clothes and tuck others into the hamper.

"That's okay." Agent Riley quickly went through the rooms with his "sniffer." It remained lifeless. "They prob-ably wore gloves. We picked up some prints downstairs, but we don't know yet whose they are. They could just be yours. We'll want to take your prints to compare."

"Of course," Mrs. White said. "We'll do anything to help end this as quickly as possible. Do you know why this is happening?"

"We've no idea, Mrs. White, but we'll find out." After a brief glance into the hall closet, agent Riley added, "I think that's all up here. Richard and I'll look around outside and be back to ask a few more questions."

While the men inspected the outside of the house and the yard, Mrs. White brewed a fresh pot of coffee. She set out mugs and a plate of cookies, nervously arranging and rearranging them on the table.

Stacey watched for a while, then wandered into the den. The room looked as it had before. The agents hadn't set anything straight. Restraining an impulse to search for the bug, she leaned on the door jamb and stared at the litter on the desk.

Were Neva Boyce, Charlie Place, and Arnold Tensley responsible for the chaos? Were they after information on Dad's current project, or were they still thinking they'd find a way to locate him? None of it made sense. They could have talked to him several times over by now. Why break in here?

Or was this a totally unrelated incident? She turned as the two agents came back into the house.

"How many telephone lines do you have?" asked agent Riley.

"Three." Stacey gestured to the phone on the desk.

"That one, one in the kitchen, and one in the hall upstairs. Why?"

"Are they all the same number?"

"Yes."

The two men exchanged glances. "Where's your mother?"

"In the kitchen. She made some coffee."

"That sounds good." Richard's faced beamed with pleasure. "Nothing like a brisk cup of coffee to get the brain working."

Stacey led them to the kitchen.

"Come have a cup of coffee and a chocolate cookie," Mrs. White invited. "What did you find?"

"No sign of forced entry. No footprints or broken shrubbery." Agent Riley pulled back a chair and sat down, stretching out his legs. "That means they found a door unlocked or picked a lock."

Coffee slopped over the rim of the cup Mrs. White was filling. She jerked around to stare at the agent. "You mean they can come in any time and—and do anything?" Her voice rose to a higher pitch.

Stacey took the coffee pot from her mother and finished pouring coffee. She set the mugs on the table and pushed the cookie plate toward agent Dicks, who'd been eyeing them hungrily.

He helped himself to a fistful and took a big bite out of one. A crumb danced at the corner of his mouth as he spoke reassuringly to Mrs. White. "We'll be watching the house. If Mr. Arthur thinks it wise, we may have a female agent come to stay for a while."

Agent Riley nodded agreement. "Mrs. White, your daughter—"

"Stacey," Mrs. White said deliberately.

"Stacey said you have three telephones in the house. But how many different lines? Is there a phone somewhere that has a different number? One your husband uses for business?"

"No. We keep telling everyone there is no special number." Mrs. White leaned her forehead on her hand. "Why can't we convince you?"

"No. I didn't mean that," explained Riley. "I was asking if you had two different telephone lines, two separate numbers in the house."

"Oh," Mrs. White relaxed some. "No. There's only one number. All three phones are the same."

"Then someone has also put a tap on the phone. We found an additional line strung over to the house."

A picture of two men in the early morning hours popped into Stacey's thoughts. "I saw them!" she exclaimed.

All eyes focused on her. "Last Thursday morning," she went on. "I was leaving the house about four-thirty to go bird watching. One man was carrying a ladder. He dropped it and bent down to pick it up. The other was up on the pole."

"Could you describe either one?" Agent Dicks popped a cookie into his mouth and grabbed up his pen.

"Both wore gray coveralls. I got the impression the one with the ladder was fairly tall and his hair was dark. The other one was shorter, heavier. I caught just a glimpse of him, and I'm not sure I'd recognize him again, but his face was round and kind of squashed. You know, kind of like a bulldog's."

"Good—can you remember anything else?"

Stacey shook her head. "It was early, pretty dark yet, and I was worried about something else. I thought they were telephone repairmen and was glad I didn't have to work that early in the morning."

"If the one man carried a ladder, they must have had a vehicle of some sort," prompted agent Riley.

"Yes. A gray panel truck. It was parked along the street." Stacey frowned. "I didn't look for the license number."

"Was there printing on the truck, a business name?"

After a moment, Stacey shook her head. "No. It was plain."

After a few more questions, fingerprinting, and a couple of common sense safety instructions, the two agents left, promising to get word back to them as soon as they knew anything.

When they were alone, Mrs. White sank back into her chair, failing to do her usual fussy cleaning up. Stacey looked at her with concern. "It's not so bad, Mom. The agents seem to know what they're doing."

"Yes, I saw that. But I can't shake this feeling of impending disaster. I wish your dad were home. I'd feel so much better."

Stacey picked up the cups and rinsed them in the sink. "We'll do okay. And if you're really uncomfortable, we can ask for an agent to move in."

"A stranger in the house?"

"Don't you think you'd feel safer, more secure?"

"What could she do?"

"I suppose she's trained to do all kinds of things. Let's wait until the agents make their suggestions. They'll take care of us." She broke off as the phone rang. Mrs. White started to rise, a frown crinkling her forehead. "Sit still, Mom. I'll get it."

"Hello?"

"Stacey White?"

"Yes."

"This is Alice Mayfair, from the church. I talked with you Sunday when you came forward."

"Oh, yes. What did you find out about my baptism?"

"No definite answer, because the senior pastor is out of town. But the associate pastor and a couple of the elders were reluctant to let your friend baptize you. They suggested that the youth pastor might do it at your Thursday night meeting. That would keep it close to your request."

"Can I think about it for a while?"

"Of course. When you decide, you can call either me

or the youth pastor and make arrangements."

"Thanks."

While Stacey talked, Mrs. White tidied the kitchen. Now she looked at Stacey, a question in her eyes.

"Someone from the church," Stacey answered the un-spoken query, something she'd never done before. "I had asked if Becky could baptize me, but they decided it had to be a pastor."

Mrs. White nodded. "Doesn't the minister always do it?"

"I don't know. I just thought it would be neat if Becky could since she's the one who kept talking to me about Jesus." Stacey walked to the door, then turned back. "Mom? Do you have a Bible?"

"I think so," Mrs. White said, surprised. "Look on the bookshelves in the den."

"Okay. They're starting a new study tomorrow night, and I thought I'd read about it first so I'd know what's going on."

"I'll help you find it, then I'll see if I can straighten out your father's desk."

After a few minutes' search, they came up with a white leather-bound Bible. Mrs. White held it a moment, a fara-way look in her eyes. "I received this at my confirmation. It meant so much to me then." She sighed and handed the book to Stacey. "Strange how some things get put aside and forgotten."

Stacey fingered the fine grained leather, her nail tracing the words "Holy Bible" stamped on the cover in gold. "Maybe it's time to come back to it."

"Maybe. But you first. Perhaps when you're finished, I'll read a little, too."

Stacey ran upstairs and changed into shorts and a halter. She creamed her face and applied sun lotion and then went to stretch out on the chaise lounge in the back yard. Opening the Bible, she searched the table of contents for the Song of Solomon.

Eagerly she found the page and began to read.

"The song of songs, which is Solomon's. Let him kiss me with the kisses of his mouth: for thy love is better than wine."

Ah, a love story, Stacey thought. She read on:

"Because of the savour of thy good ointments thy name is as ointment poured forth, therefore do the virgins love thee. Draw me, we will run after thee: the king hath brought me into his chambers: we will be glad and rejoice in thee, we will remember thy love more than wine: the upright love thee. I am black but comely . . ."

Stacey skimmed through the rest of the first chapter. It didn't make sense. Was it because of the funny old language?

With her finger stuck in the place, she rubbed the book across her cheek bone. Maybe she'd go buy her own Bible, one with modern language like Becky suggested.

Following her thoughts with action, she jumped up and hurried to her room. After showering, she pulled on a tee shirt and matching shorts. She went down to the den where her mother was sorting through the chaos. "Here's your Bible, Mom. I'm going downtown for a while."

"Finished reading so soon?" Mrs. White gestured at the piles of stuff scattered over the desk. "I've hardly made a dent in this."

"I didn't understand much. I guess I'll wait for the class. I'll be here for dinner."

"We need to eat early—about five—so I can get to work."

"I'll take the Chevy so I can be back on time."

"Thanks, dear."

Stacey pulled into the parking lot at the Open Door book store just as Erica got out of her car.

Erica waited for Stacey to join her. "Are you already finding a need for books to help? I think I've been their best customer since I became a Christian."

"I'm looking for a Bible. All I have is a New Testament

that Becky gave me. You heard we're going to study in the Old Testament tomorrow night?"

"Yes," Erica replied, "I tried to read the book, but it didn't make sense. I thought I'd see if they have something that would help explain it."

Stacey felt relieved that she wasn't the only one having a difficult time with the book. "I thought it was just me— or the old Bible of mother's I tried to read."

"The old version may have had something to do with it, but I have a modern language Bible, and I'm still having trouble. What version are you going to get?"

"I don't know." Stacey lifted her hands in a helpless gesture. "I don't know enough about anything to even choose. Tell me about what you have."

"Bob, the store owner, will help. He helped me pick out a Bible that was easy to read. Let's ask."

During the next half hour, Stacey and Erica looked over several different Bibles, while Bob gave suggestions and pointed out features of each.

"Look at this one," he urged. "In addition to the foot-notes and cross references, it has mini-articles on various subjects as they're dealt with in the Bible. Here's one on tithing," he flipped a couple of pages, "one on forgiveness, and another on baptism."

"Oh, that reminds me," Stacey said to Erica. "I think I'll ask the youth pastor to baptize me at one of the Thursday night classes."

"Can you do that?"

"Yes. I got a call from the church today suggesting it. I wanted Becky to since she's the one who kept telling me about Jesus, but they thought it should be a pastor."

"Stacey, let's be baptized together. How about tomorrow night?"

"Tomorrow?"

"Sure. If we call today, I don't see why we can't do it tomorrow night." Excitement squeaked in her voice. "Let's."

"Okay." Stacey's eyes brightened. "In fact, yes! I think that would be super. I'll call Mrs. Mayfair when I get home."

Stacey selected a Bible bound in burgundy leather. "I only have twenty dollars with me," she told Bob. "Will you hold it for me until I get more money from Mom!"

"Sure. In fact, you can take it now. Do you want your name engraved on the front?"

"I did," said Erica. "If I lose it, it'll always come home."

"It's free," Bob offered.

"I'd like that." She wrote her name as she wanted it on the Bible: Stacey C. White.

Bob added a delicate butterfly design and said, "It takes about ten minutes."

While they waited, they browsed through the study books, but didn't find anything on the Song of Solomon that looked understandable.

"I guess we'll just have to wait to see what Ken Masters says about it," Erica decided. "Mike met him a couple of months ago and was really impressed with what Ken told him about the book. As I recall, Mike said he had a totally different approach from most teachers."

At home, Mrs. White had a light supper of soup, salad and crusty french bread waiting. As they sat down to eat, she said, "I hate leaving you here alone. I'm worried about someone breaking in."

"I'll be okay. Did agent Riley call?"

"Yes. They had nothing to report yet, but he told me they'd leave the bug in place for a while at least. They also want to leave the tap on the phone."

Stacey groaned, hitting her cheekbones with the palms of her hands. "The phone tap. Oh no!"

"What's the matter?" her mother queried.

"Remember when I told Dad about my conversation with Charlie on our old cabin? My whole intent was to send them on a wild goose chase. But if they're the ones who tapped the phone, they heard the conversation. They'll know I led him on."

Immediately Stacey was sorry she'd mentioned it. A deeper worry settled on her mother's face.

"They'll be angry, maybe vengeful," she fretted.

"Oh, Mom," Stacey tried to reassure her. "They'll be so busy trying to find whatever it is they want that they'll never bother with me. They'll probably take it as a joke or be glad they found out before they trudged around looking for the cabin." But her words carried no reassurance for her mother. The worried look stayed.

The next night, the group gathered in the first few rows of the main sanctuary to see Stacey and Erica be baptized. Erica went first. Stacey watched as the pastor asked Erica if she believed in Jesus, dipped her in the water, and raised her up again.

It was her turn. All of a sudden she felt conspicuous and vulnerable. What would everyone think?

Those thoughts vanished as the pastor asked, "Stacey, do you believe that Jesus is the Christ, the Son of God?"

"Yes."

"Have you accepted Him as your Savior, trusting Him to take away your sins and give you eternal life?"

"I have."

"I baptize you in the name of the Father, of the Son, and of the Holy Spirit."

Then she was under water. As the pastor lifted her up, she heard him say, ". . . and raised to new life in Jesus Christ."

She smiled tremulously as the group started to sing, "They have decided to follow Jesus. No turning back."

She looked out toward the group. Her eyes widened in disbelief as they met the eyes of the photographer from the woods. His grin stretched almost from ear to ear. Her lids snapped shut. What was he doing here?

Chapter Eight

Stacey made a conscious effort to forget about the grinning photographer in the crowd. Despite the fact that he'd been laughing at her—and she'd concluded Friday morning he was the kind who would laugh if she explained why she'd been crying—joy bubbled deep inside.

What did one clumsy, noisy photographer matter when she had Jesus in her heart? When she'd been obedient and followed His command to be baptized?

Back in the dressing room, Erica said, "I've never felt quite like this before. Sort of excited and happy, but serious and reverent at the same time."

"Me, too." Stacey wrapped a towel turban-style around her head before taking off the wet baptismal gown. She quickly changed back into her blue cords with a white, fleecy sweat shirt. "I feel like an all-new person. Will it last?"

"From what I've learned from Mrs. Havig, yes. Not always to the same degree. It depends on how obedient we are to what we know Christ wants us to do."

"Like we did tonight?"

"Yes. But Mrs. Havig stressed that we can't depend on our feelings. We need to trust that what God said is true, regardless of how we feel."

Both girls turned on blow dryers. Soon Stacey's black hair lay smooth and neat, swinging loosely as she leaned toward the mirror to refresh her lipstick.

Erica put down her dryer. "I wish I could wear my hair like yours. Does a single strand ever get out of place?"

"Of course. I just comb it back again. It's naturally easy to take care of—especially since I had it cut this way."

"Lucky you." Erica said, zipping her sports bag. "Ready?"

Stacey drew in a deep breath. Remembering the mocking grin on the photographer's face, she almost felt like going home. But she decided she wouldn't miss out on the new study because of him. "I guess so."

They hurried up the stairs to the old balcony. They climbed halfway up the raised tiers and took two places Mike had saved for them.

"For the benefit of those who are new tonight," Mike announced from the podium, "we're introducing ourselves. Ted and Nancy in the back row are next and then you two."

While Ted, Nancy, and Erica told their names, where they lived, and their favorite ice cream flavors, Stacey looked around, curious to identify the new teacher. In the third row across the room was the guy from the woods. His gray-green eyes met hers. He winked.

She looked away, and continued her search for the new teacher. She decided it must be the pudgy fellow sitting in the front row, clasping a big, worn Bible.

Then it was her turn. She dropped the writing arm of her chair and stood. "I'm Stacey White. Many of you know me as Carolyn, but since graduation, I've decided to go by my first name—Stacey. I live here in Karston and my favorite ice cream is licorice."

Across the room the blond photographer signaled an approving okay with circled thumb and forefinger.

Mike continued the program. "Now that we know a little about each other, let's get into our new study."

A shuffling sound filled the room as everyone eased around in their chairs and pulled out Bibles and notebooks.

"My new friend, Ken Masters, has recently moved to

Karston. He's so excited about what he's learned through studying the Song of Solomon that he hooked me. So our committee got together and asked him to share with our group.

"Ken's attending the University of Washington, majoring in business administration. He's originally from Oregon and we're glad that he's with us tonight. The rest of the time is yours, Ken."

Stacey looked expectantly at the pudgy stranger in the front row, expecting him to move to the front and plant his big Bible on the lectern. He just twisted in his seat and watched as the blond fellow from the woods made his way down the steps.

Him? The photographer who laughed at her? The guy she'd yelled at twice? The one she knew she had to apologize to someday? This was worse than ever. She slid down in her seat, hoping to be less conspicuous.

Ken smiled at everyone as he picked up a notebook from the table and opening it, laid it on the lectern. "I can't think of a better way to start this study on the Song of Solomon than with a baptism."

"My Aunt Ruby used this book to teach me Christian discipleship. Baptism is one of those things—a step of obedience to Christ, a symbol of our death to the old things and our birth into a new life in God."

He looked up at Stacey and Erica. "Thank you for choosing tonight to be baptized. Let's thank God, too." He bowed his head. "Father, thank you for a perfect beginning for our study. Now I ask that you'll give me the right words to share what has become so meaningful to me. I ask in Jesus' name, Amen."

Ken's gaze touched everyone in the balcony. He smiled. "You are quite a shock to me. I guess I forgot to ask Mike how large your group is. I had envisioned a small, cozy group gathered around a table. Instead I get a roomful. I feel like I should be a preacher."

He paused while a ripple of laughter circled the room.

"But I'm not. So we'll go on as though we were a small group. I expect a lot of give and take in this study, with discussion, questions, role playing: whatever works best to learn these important lessons.

"As I said, I got my knowledge from my aunt, Ruby McFarling. She's a very special lady who has devoted over twenty years to studying the Song of Solomon and using what she has discovered to help others live better Christian lives."

Stacey glanced around the room. Everyone was leaning forward, eager to follow Ken's teaching.

"The Song of Solomon is composed like a symphony. Yet, in some ways, it is also like an opera, with a plot and a cast of characters. Let me introduce you.

"The hero is a king. A handsome man. He's wise, observant, sensitive, loving. In the book, he's called 'my beloved.' He is our Savior, the Lord Jesus Christ."

He grinned. "The heroine is a fair-to-middlin' good-looking woman. At first, she makes some mistakes and has much to learn, but as the king loves and encourages her, she grows, matures, and becomes more beautiful. She has lots of names: 'my love,' 'my dove,' 'my undefiled,' 'my sister,' or 'my spouse' by the king and 'the fairest among women' by a chorus of weak Christians called 'the daughters of Jerusalem.' She represents one member of the body of Christ—any member.

"There are other characters, but we'll get to them and learn their names and their counterparts in our world as they appear in the script."

Stacey sat spellbound as he continued to share information about the book. What had made no sense at all to her, even in her new study Bible, became clear as Ken explained.

When he left the podium, Stacey leaned back and looked at Erica. "That was good. I'm amazed that all of what he said is in those verses I couldn't understand."

"I know. I took notes like mad. This is going to be a

great study." Erica smiled. "I'm glad you're here. I heard you might go to Denver with your dad."

"I wasn't very happy when it didn't work out to go, but this study will make up for it; especially if I can find a job." Stacey stood and picked up her Bible and notebook. "I guess I'll head for home."

"Why don't you come out for a Coke with us. We usually go to the Shanty and talk things over after the meetings."

Stacey hesitated only a moment. "Sure. I'd love to. Shall I meet you there?"

"Yes, but hang around for a while. Someone might need a ride. I need to make sure my kid brother has a way home. See you in a few minutes."

Stacey felt awkward standing around. How would anyone know she was going to the Shanty and could take them? Maybe she should just go. She was sidling toward the door when Becky came up and threw her arms around Stacey.

"You're always surprising me. Last week, you make a decision for Christ without letting me in on it and tonight the baptism." She hugged Stacey again. "I'm so happy for you."

"Me, too," said a deep, familiar voice from behind Stacey. "Congratulations." Ken Masters held out a large hand. "Welcome into the family of God."

Stacey felt her hand swallowed up in his big warm one. He held it while she introduced Becky, almost as though he'd forgotten to let go. It was a comforting grasp, not a spine tingling caress like Charlie had given.

Her hand felt cold when he released it to shake hands with Becky. She couldn't help noticing that he didn't hold hers.

"Are you two going to the Shanty?" he asked.

"Yes," said Stacey. "How about you Becky?"

"Just so happens I can. Dondra is taking care of things at home tonight."

"Do you need a ride?" Stacey reached in her bag for her car keys. "I'm driving."

"I have my car. I'll meet you there." Becky swung her key ring around her finger. "Guess we didn't plan very well."

"Neither did I," Ken put in. "I walked to the church." His gray-green eyes laughed down into Stacey's. "Do you suppose I could tag along with you?"

For an instant, apprehension at being alone with him choked off her voice. *May as well get it over with*, she told herself. "S-Sure. I think everyone's heading that way. Shall we go?"

The three of them walked out to the parking lot. Ken and Stacey left Becky at her car. Stacey climbed into her old Chevy and reached over to unlock the other door.

For a few moments starting the car and easing into traffic kept her busy, but then she knew she had to apologize.

"I think I—" she started, her voice lapping over his.

He laughed. "Ladies first."

"I don't know how to say this, except to blurt it out." Stacey glanced over at his puzzled face. "I owe you an apology—two of them. I was really rude to you out in the woods. I'd like you to forgive me."

"Accepted, particularly since I was about to apologize for butting in on your quiet on those two occasions."

She looked over at him again. "You have as much right there as I do. That first morning, I was terribly disappointed. I'd counted on getting to go to Denver for the summer. My father is working on a special project there, and I wanted to go along. He couldn't take me."

"That'd be a real letdown," Ken sympathized. "I know how awful disappointment can be."

She hesitated, then added shyly, "The second time, I'd just invited Jesus into my heart. I knew I must look terrible and I'm afraid vanity—or something—made me flip out."

Ken reached out and patted her hand on the steering wheel. "Forgiven and forgotten. But tell me, what were you looking for that I scared off?"

"*Psaltriparus minimus*. I call them mini's. They're not

a rare bird, just hard to spot. I've heard them a lot, but haven't actually identified one by sight to add to my life list."

"When did you get interested in birds?"

"A couple of years ago. Our neighbors added a feeder and bird bath to their back yard. I couldn't help noticing all the different kinds of birds that came, and I got curious as to what they all were."

"I haven't gotten much into identification. I just like to find a natural setting and see what wildlife I can capture on film. I've been experimenting with light and shadow and trying some new effects."

"I'd like to see your pictures." Stacey pulled into the parking lot at the Shanty.

"We'll have to get together. Maybe you can identify some of the birds for me."

Mike, Erica, and Becky were in their special booth. Ken's hand rested lightly on Stacey's back as they made their way through the crowd.

Stacey was about to sit down when a frown crossed her face. "Excuse me a minute," she said. "I think I'd better call Mom. She'll be worried since I didn't tell her I'd be late." Looking back over her shoulder, she added, "Go ahead and order. I like anything except anchovy."

When she got back to the booth, Ken stood, letting her slide in next to Erica.

"Everything okay?" Erica asked.

"Fine."

Under cover of the others' discussion about the lesson, Erica said, "I don't mean to pry, but last time we were out, you mentioned your mom didn't care about when you got in. Something change?"

Stacey hesitated, wondering how much to share. "Some strange things have been happening," she confided, "and Mom worries about everything now."

Ken leaned close to Stacey, "Anything we should pray about?"

"Pray about?"

"Yes. Jesus wants us to share all our cares with Him. He can handle them better than we can."

"Well, maybe." Stacey looked around the table as they all watched her. "I guess I can tell you. No one said anything about it being confidential."

Their pizza number was called, and Ken jumped up to get it. "Wait 'til I'm back."

Simply, without dramatics, Stacey outlined everything that had happened: the men at the airport, the phone calls, tapping the phone, the date with Charlie, the ransacked desks, the CIA agents.

When she finished, Mike said, "Another mystery. Boy. Do I run with the right crowd." He smiled at Stacey. "We may have to enlarge our ranks a bit. Is that all right?"

"What do you mean?"

"Well, to solve the last mystery and catch Tyson, we had Fred and Leslie to help—but the best sleuth of all is Alex, Erica's little brother. If we brought him in on it, we could probably find out what those guys want and resolve the matter before the CIA does."

Erica groaned. "Don't tell Alex. I don't think we could take his involvement in another mystery. He almost wound up in jail last time."

"He's smarter now," Mike teased. "He knows what not to do."

Erica made a face at him.

"I don't know," Stacey back-pedaled. "I'm sure agent Riley wouldn't like it. They definitely don't want the local police in on it, so I'm sure he wouldn't be thrilled with a bunch of kids getting in the way."

"Maybe you're right," Mike admitted. "But if there's anything we can do, let us know."

"We can pray about it." Ken grasped Stacey's hand, then reached across the table to take Becky's. "Join hands and let's pray right now."

After a moment of silence, he prayed, "Father, You

know what is going on and why these people are so insistent on finding Stacey's dad. We know from the things they're doing that they are not within the law nor do they have good intentions. We ask that You overrule and let right win. Protect Stacey, her mother and her father. And, Lord, if there's anything the rest of us can do, make it clear to us. Amen."

"Can I give you a ride home?" Stacey offered Ken as everyone got ready to leave.

"Thanks, but Mike goes right past my place." He called to Mike. "Do you think we should follow Stacey home? Make sure she gets there okay?"

"Good idea."

"That's not necessary," Stacey protested. "I'm not in any danger."

"Sure you feel comfortable driving through town alone?"

"Of course. I've done it hundreds of times."

Ken walked her to her car. "Would you consider going to the woods together some morning? I'd promise to be quiet."

Stacey grinned. "I was an old ogre, wasn't I? I'd love to go. And I promise not to yell."

"It's a deal. How about Saturday?"

"Five-thirty?"

"I'll pick you up."

Stacey slid into the driver's seat and Ken closed the door behind her. "Take care, Stacey. See you Saturday."

When Stacey got home, the ground floor was ablaze with lights. She put the car in the garage and dashed to the kitchen door.

Her mother met her and threw her arms around her. "Oh, Stacey! I'm so glad you're all right." She drew back, almost frightened by her unaccustomed display of emotion. "I was so worried. Thanks for calling. If I hadn't just heard from you, I would have been frantic."

"Why? What happened?"

"About a half hour after you called, the phone rang again. When I answered, a muffled voice asked if I knew where you were." Her hands twisted together. "I almost told them, but I stopped myself in time. I only said that I did know."

"Is that all they wanted to know?"

"No. They asked if I knew where Doug was. I said, 'of course.' The voice said, 'We know where they are, too.' Then the line went dead."

"Did you call agent Riley?"

"Yes. He said there wasn't anything they could do to-night. He asked where you were and who you were with. He was going to try to get agent Dicks over to escort you home. Did you see him?"

"No, though a car followed me. I thought it was Mike and Erica. They'd talked about it—and prayed for us. See, Mom, it's going to be all right."

"Well, the agents are coming over tomorrow morning to tell us what they want us to do. They'll be here about eight-thirty."

When they arrived the next morning, agent Riley asked, "Any more phone calls?"

"No." Mrs. White perched on the edge of a kitchen chair. "Do you think there'll be more?"

"We can't tell. We're working with your husband and his Denver contact to determine what this is all about." Riley leaned back and stretched out his legs. "So far, none of us can find a reason. Until we do, we're working in the dark."

"You called Doug?"

"Yes, after we talked last night. Everything's normal at that end. I think the only thing we accomplished was to make him worry about you."

His pleasant expression faded as he glanced at Stacey. "Could one of your friends think such a phone call would be a joke?"

"No." Stacey shook her head vigorously. "The only people I told about any of this were the ones I was with last night—when Mom got the phone."

"What did you tell them?"

"Just about what has happened."

Riley stroked his chin. "Did you think it might not be wise?"

"I considered it, but they're all my friends. They're all straight. In fact, when I finished, they prayed with me about it."

"Prayed?" echoed Riley.

"That's right, asking for God's protection and a quick resolution."

Agent Dicks grinned at Stacey. "That gets him every time. The boss hasn't figured Christians out yet."

Mrs. White jumped as the phone rang. She rose to answer it. She listened for a moment. The blood drained from her face, leaving her chalky white. Then she crumpled to the floor, the dangling receiver swaying above her inert body.

Chapter Nine

Agent Dicks grabbed the phone with his left hand. His right reached for Mrs. White's throat to feel for a pulse. Agent Riley headed at a dead run for the phone in the den, motioning Stacey to take the kitchen receiver.

A whispery voice rasped in Stacey's ear. "Did you hear me?"

"What did you say to my mother?" she demanded.

"Stacey? Is that you?"

"This is Stacey. Who are you?"

"That doesn't matter. Just remind your mother that if she doesn't cooperate, we'll be sending her that parcel." A harsh, joyless laugh ended the conversation.

"Mrs. White . . . Mrs. White." Agent Dicks stopped rubbing her wrists and patted her not too gently on her cheek. "Can you hear me?"

Stacey dropped to her knees. "Mom," she pleaded. "Mom, wake up." She looked tearfully up at Riley. "She's never passed out before. What do we do?"

"Do you have any ammonia?"

She nodded.

"Douse a rag with some and bring it here."

Stacey raced for the cleaning closet. She heard Riley ask Richard Dicks, "She has only fainted, hasn't she?" She held her breath, waiting for the answer.

"I think so. There's a fairly strong pulse, but it's irregular. Could be . . ." his voice faded into a whisper.

Grabbing a clean rag, she splashed the acrid solution generously over it and hurried back, tears smarting her eyes from the fumes.

Agent Dicks reached for the rag. "Ugh. That's powerful." He held it close to Mrs. White's nose.

She gasped and choked. Her lids fluttered open. Her pale blue eyes, wild and frightened, searched until they rested on Stacey. "Call your dad. See if he's all right."

"Sure, Mom. But are you okay?"

"Don't waste time." Somehow Mrs. White put fire in her weak voice. "Call now!"

Stacey looked to Riley.

He nodded. "I'll put a call through."

While he flipped through his notebook looking for the number, Dicks helped Mrs. White up and guided her into the living room. Stacey walked beside her mother, holding her hand.

Propping a couple of pillows under her mother's head and tucking an afghan around her, Stacey asked, "Should I call Doctor Andies? Are you okay?"

"I'll be fine as soon as I talk to Doug." Mrs. White's hand shook as she brushed a wisp of hair back from her forehead. Her face looked almost savage as she glared at Dicks. "Why is this happening to us? Why?"

He was saved from answering by Riley's return.

"Mr. White is in the lab now. I talked to Mr. Arthur." Riley smiled soothingly at Mrs. White. "He talked by intercom to your husband. He'll call in about an hour."

Mrs. White pushed herself upright. "Are you sure? Was he really there? Did you hear his voice?"

"Mom! Mr. Arthur wouldn't lie."

"I'm not so sure." Mrs. White slumped back against the pillows. "Was he there?"

Riley sat down across from Mrs. White. He eased his right ankle over his left knee and tapped his pen on the sole

of his shoe. "I've no reason to disbelieve Mr. Arthur. If your
husband wasn't there, he wouldn't promise a phone call
within an hour."

Some of the tension drained from Mrs. White's face.
Her expression was more puzzled than angry when she repeated, "Why is this happening? Is it because Stacey dated
that awful man?"

"No. It started long before then." He smiled at Stacey.
"I think Stacey is aware that he asked her simply to see what
he could find out from her."

Stacey nodded. "I suspected that; it was so obvious
when he started asking certain questions. I thought I'd led
him on a wild goose chase, but spoiled it all when I bragged
about it to Dad."

He lifted an eyebrow in question.

"If they're the ones tapping the phone, they heard Dad
say we'd sold the cabin years ago."

"Cabin?" put in Dicks.

Stacey explained her conversation with Charlie.

Dicks grinned. "Good try. Too bad about the phone
tap."

Mrs. White frowned. "Won't they try to get even?"

"I doubt whether it's important enough," soothed Riley.
"And, to answer your earlier question, we don't know why
they're bothering you. We're still looking. It may help if we
knew what that phone call was about. Can you talk about
it?"

Color rushed to Mrs. White's face, then drained away,
leaving her almost as white as when she fainted. "The voice
was awful. Whispery. I couldn't tell if it was a man or a
woman."

"I wasn't sure either." Stacey shivered as she looked at
Riley. "Could you tell?"

He shook his head. "You didn't recognize anything
about the voice?"

"No." Mrs. White was definite.

"What shook you up so badly?"

"He—she—whoever—told me that if I didn't cooperate, they'd . . ."

Agent Dicks reached out to steady Mrs. White, grasping her hand.

Sobs began to shake her shoulders. "They said they'd . . . send me the . . ." her voice choked, "the little finger of someone I loved. That I could . . . I could k-keep it as a memento."

With a cry, Stacey knelt beside her mother. "Mom. No one would do that. Not today." She twisted to look at the agents. "It's not possible?"

Agent Riley remained noncommittal, but agent Dicks shook his head. "Most likely scare tactics. Trying to soften you up for whatever demand they're going to make."

The phone shrilled into the following silence. Stacey rose to answer.

Mrs. White's voice followed her. "If it's Doug, I must talk with him."

"Okay, Mom." She lifted the receiver. "White residence. Yes. Yes. When?" She glanced at her watch. "Yes, I can be there. Thank you."

Her step was a little lighter as she returned to the living room. "That was a job offer. From Dad's office! I didn't even consider applying there. They want me to come in at two this afternoon for orientation, then start work Monday."

The two agents exchanged a smile. "That's great," said Dicks. "Seems I remember you've been job hunting."

"I've scoured the town and there's been nothing. This is great!" A glance at her mother's drawn face dampened her enthusiasm. She knelt by her mother's chair. "I know you're terribly worried, Mom; but let's be glad over a bit of good news."

Mrs. White smiled and patted Stacey's shoulder. "I am pleased. I know it's what you want." A tremor shook her body, and she wiped her brow with a shaking hand. "I just thought . . ." Her blue eyes were almost white with terror. "What if they didn't mean Doug? What if they meant one of our older children or one of our grandchildren?''

Riley laid a soothing hand on her arm. "That's been taken care of. Mr. White insisted that we contact your other children and warn them of possible danger. He felt a little worry was better than risking violence." He patted her arm again. "Each one has been contacted and agents are keeping a check on them."

"Do you really think they're in danger?" Stacey turned to look at Dicks. She'd learned that his face revealed his thoughts much more than Riley's.

"Negative. It's only a precaution." He smiled. "The CIA follows grandma's old rule: 'It's better to be safe than sorry.' "

Stacey grinned back at him. "Sounds good to me."

The agents spent a little more time reassuring Mrs. White and then left.

Stacey wished she could do something to make her mother feel better. If only she could pray with her mother like Ken prayed last night, but she'd never prayed aloud. Instead she said, "If you're okay, Mom, I'll get ready for my job appointment."

"Fine. I'll just rest here for a while."

Stacey ran upstairs. Before getting ready to shower, she knelt by her bed. "Father," she prayed, "don't let these evil people hurt any of my family. They've threatened us, but I've learned that You are all powerful and in control. Don't let them do it."

Feeling somehow calmer, she showered and took care choosing an outfit that would be businesslike—a blue suede skirt and a white tailored blouse. She applied a soft color to her cheeks, mascara, and a touch of lipstick.

Her mother looked up as she reentered the living room. "You look very nice, Car . . . Stacey. I've been reading." She waved the white confirmation Bible, her finger tucked between two pages. "I remember some of this. I memorized it when I was in grade school. Listen."

She opened the Bible and read, " 'God is our refuge and

strength, a very present help in trouble. Therefore will not we fear, though the earth be removed, and though the mountains be carried into the midst of the sea.' "

Her voice stumbled to a halt. "I guess you think I'm foolish."

Stacey wanted to take her mother in her arms and reassure her, but the habit of restraint was strong. Instead, she said, "No, Mom. Perhaps we're just becoming wise. Maybe we should have turned to God for help a long time ago."

Mrs. White put down the Bible. "I made a spinach, apple and bacon salad. Are you ready to eat?"

"Ummm. Yes. That's my favorite."

Stacey dished up the salad while Mrs. White heated dinner rolls and laid out the table settings.

They ate almost in silence, with only a word now and then. When they were about done, Mrs. White said, "Stacey, I don't understand what has changed you, but I like it. For the first time in years, I feel that you and I are on the same wavelength. Thank you for being kind, for . . . for, well, for acting as if you cared."

Stacey felt the old anger surge, resentment that her mother would invade her private feelings. But before it could escape, something nudged her, reminding her of the fact that she needed to ask her mother's forgiveness for not doing her part to maintain a good relationship.

Stacey gulped back an emotion that threatened to close off her voice and said, "I'm not sure I can explain, Mom. Last Friday I asked Jesus to come into my heart. He did. He forgave all my sins, because I asked Him to. And now, I think He wants me to ask you to forgive me, too. Will you?"

Tears glistened in the eyes of both as they reached across the table and clasped hands.

"Oh, yes, Stacey—and I need your forgiveness, too," Mrs. White said softly. "I haven't been the mother to you I was to the older children. I guess I felt you knew all the things I worked so hard to instill in the others."

"I thought it meant you didn't love me." Tears trickled down Stacey's cheeks, leaving a trail of black mascara. "That I was a nuisance who came along nine years late."

"Oh, no." Mrs. White smiled through her tears. "I must admit it was a bit of a shock when I discovered I was pregnant again. But then I felt pure joy. I knew I'd have one more child, one who would lessen the pangs when all the others grew up and left home."

A troubled look crossed her face. "I don't know when or why we didn't grow as close as I imagined we'd be. Maybe I got too involved in my job. I don't know."

"Whatever it was, it's all right. I guess I'm a person who needs some space and privacy. Maybe I've fought too hard for that, then couldn't figure out why you weren't there when I did want you." Stacey blotted her eyes and blew her nose. "Forgiven?"

"Of course." Mrs. White gave a shaky laugh and squeezed Stacey's fingers. "You'd better go repair your makeup. You'll be late for that appointment."

"Thanks, Mom. Are you working today?"

"Yes. I'll be gone when you get back. Take care, Stacey."

"I will. Oh, I'm going bird watching tomorrow. Ken, the guy that's teaching our new Bible study, is taking me. He's into photographing wildlife."

"Bring him for breakfast if you'd like."

"I'll see." Stacey dashed upstairs to repair her makeup.

When the phone rang, she heard her mother run to answer it. She walked to the top of the stairs to listen.

"Doug, is it really you?" Her mother's breath caught in a little sob. "I've been so worried. Yes. We're all right here."

Stacey listened while her mother told about the phone call this morning and the assurances of the CIA men. She gathered that her father couldn't get home for a while, that the project was in a critical phase and he couldn't leave.

She glanced at her watch and gasped. If she didn't get

moving, she'd be late. Her heart sang despite the worries of the morning as she deftly redid her mascara and headed for her appointment. Her dad was okay, and she and her mother were finally opening up to each other, starting over.

When she arrived at the lab, a receptionist showed her into the director's office, introduced her, and left. She was waved to a chair across an enormous, cluttered desk from a man with wild red hair liberally streaked with white. He was talking on the phone and scribbling notes.

She grinned inwardly. He looked like a caricature of a mad scientist in the movies. She sat in the indicated chair, making an effort to sit tall and look poised.

He smiled encouragingly at her from time to time until he finished the call. "Sorry to keep you waiting." He glanced at an open folder amid the clutter on the desk. "You're Doug White's daughter, ready to follow in his footsteps. You've got quite a goal there. Your dad's good. One of our best."

"Thank you. I'm rather partial to him myself." She smiled, and he grinned back at her, putting her at ease.

"Now, we've been looking for someone who would be willing to do odd jobs around here, small things that take up valuable time from the physicists, but are essential to the overall success of our department."

Stacey leaned forward, "You think I might be able to—"

"You're just the one," he interrupted. "You have a little knowledge in this line, you're bright, eager to learn. Just the kind of person we want. Now, if you're ready, I'll call Colin and have him show you around. Colin is our junior physicist. He'll introduce you to everyone, see that you know where everything is. He also has a list of the things we want you to take on."

He flipped a switch on his desk intercom and spoke in the same rapid fire voice. "Send in Colin. We're ready for a tour of the place."

Before Stacey could rise, he added, "Now, before he

gets here, do you have any questions?"

"Yes." Stacey decided to be as direct as he. "How about salary, hours, general rules and regulations?"

"Good questions. Those that Colin can't answer, ask my receptionist, Miss Gray. If you're still confused on anything, come see me after you start work next week. Now, one thing I can answer. Be here Monday morning, nine o'clock sharp."

A knock on the door was followed by a head and shoulders thrust through the opening. The shoulders were broad, the head covered with wavy hair as black as Stacey's.

"Colin, this is," he checked the record in front of him. "Stacey Carolyn White, Doug's daughter. I understand you are called Carolyn."

"No. Stacey."

"Stacey it is. This is Colin Trent. He's been instructed to brief you and show you the ropes."

Stacey left the office with Colin. He was at least six inches taller than Stacey and had the long slim hands of an artist.

He chuckled. "Feel like you've been through a whirl-wind?"

"As a matter of fact, that's a good comparison. Is he always like that?"

"Always. A great boss. He's open, fair, honest. But don't be misled by his bonhomie. He has standards, and he expects everyone of us to toe the mark. That includes being here on time, working hard while you're here, doing your work well and completely."

He led her along a corridor lined with doors. As they passed each one, he explained what went on inside, opening some to show her.

Over the next hour, she met a score of people and learned that she'd be doing some computer input, running errands, helping in various projects whenever a non-skilled hand was required, and generally filling in. They discussed her salary and hours. Again Colin said, "Remember, in order to be a success here—and you could keep this job through college—do what is expected of you, when it's expected of you, and do it well."

Stacey leaned back in a chair in the staff lounge where they were finishing their discussion. "I understand. I'll do my best. Could I ask one more question?"

"All you want. Then it's my turn." He smiled across at her, gray eyes twinkling.

"I had expected to see one more person here today— Neva Boyce. I understood she worked here."

The friendliness disappeared from Colin's face. It closed off like he'd slammed a door. With an apparent effort, he informed her, "As far as I know, no one of that name has ever worked here. How do you know her?"

"Oh, she came to our house one day, looking for Dad."

Some of the strain left his face, but Stacey thought she detected a calculating look in his eyes. She was almost sure neither her gleaming black hair or feminine charm prompted his next question.

"Are you free tomorrow night for dinner?"

"No." She was not going out with someone just to be an information source again. "Thanks, but I already have plans."

"Oh. Well maybe we can work in a lunch together next week."

"Maybe."

Chapter Ten

All the way home, Stacey puzzled over Colin's change of manner when she had mentioned Neva Boyce.

She had been sure his remark about being his turn to ask questions indicated he wanted to get to know her better. Although he'd asked her out, she knew his personal interest had evaporated as quickly as a thimbleful of water on a hot griddle.

She reviewed everything she could remember about Neva Boyce. Then it dawned on her. Her father had said he'd only heard of Neva, but had never met her. Neva had never worked at the lab. She'd lied about working with Doug White.

Whatever her dad and Colin had heard about Neva must have been negative. It was bad enough to make Colin think less of her because she had appeared eager to meet Neva. What was it about Neva Boyce that made people react so?

Still baffled, Stacey put the car in the garage and let herself into the house. A note written on pale lavender paper caught her eye.

She smiled as she read, "Makings for a BLT are in the refrigerator. Have a nice evening. Hope you got the job. Mom. P.S. I love you."

Humming to herself, Stacey went upstairs to change clothes. Clad in comfortable blue jeans and a white sweat shirt, Stacey sat at her desk and took out her journal. Never very consistent in keeping a day-to-day account of her activities, she did try to record the important things in her life.

She started back a couple of weeks with graduation day, bringing the record up to date. Nibbling on the end of her pen, Stacey tried to recall exactly what had happened each day. She promised herself again that she'd make writing in her journal a daily must, so it wouldn't be such a struggle.

Ending up with an account of her orientation at the lab, she included the cool reaction to Neva Boyce's name.

Stacey opened her new burgundy leather Bible to her place in Acts, read a few verses, and made notes to ask Becky about on Sunday. Then, taking the little booklet Becky had given her to read, she curled up against the pillows on her bed and opened to the first page.

The booklet had lots of good information. Stacey's attention was drawn to a little diagram showing how to have assurance of salvation. It encompassed three things: belief in the trustworthiness of God's Word, which says we are saved if we believe in Jesus; an assurance from the Holy Spirit who now dwells within us and tells us we're children of God; and a changed life.

Stacey put the booklet down. She did believe—she'd talked it over with the counselor at church. She was all right on that point, but she had questions about the Holy Spirit within. She wasn't sure she understood completely, but it could be the joy and lightness she'd experienced since asking Jesus into her life—maybe even the promptings to ask forgiveness, to curb her anger. And her mother had mentioned her changed life.

She bowed her head. "Thank you, Jesus, for saving me. I'm sure I'm a Christian. Give me the desire to do Your will, to be obedient to what You command."

Before she went down to fix her supper, she put a few things away she had carelessly tossed aside and even dusted the furniture.

The doorbell rang as she headed downstairs. She

checked through the peephole, then swung the door wide. Erica, Mike, and Ken all grinned at her.

"We're in search of something fun to do this evening," Erica said.

"And we decided we needed you to make our quest a success," added Ken. A frown flitted across his face. "You are free, aren't you?"

Stacey laughed and invited them in. "Yes, I'm free and something fun to do is just what I need." She led them into the living room. "What ideas do you have?"

"We thought of going to a movie, renting a movie, watching TV . . ."

"All about as exciting as watching paint peel," Ken interrupted Mike. "We were hoping you were more inspired than the rest of us."

"For starters, have you eaten? I, for one, am famished."

Mike hit his temples with doubled up hands. "Now, why couldn't we have thought of something so clever?"

"Maybe because we're so hungry we can't think," quipped Erica. "What would you like? Pizza, hamburgers, Mexican?"

Stacey looked from face to face. None of Erica's suggestions seemed to hit it big with either Mike or Ken. She worried a moment about how she'd feel if they turned down her suggestion, then noticed Ken looking at her with a twinkle in his eye.

"She has another idea. Out with it, Stacey."

"Mom left ingredients for BLT's in the refrigerator. Want to rough it and cook your own?"

Ken shook his head, and Stacey's heart sank.

"Can't do that," he said. "But you and Erica can do the fixing. Mike and I will eat."

"No way." Stacey stood and cracked an imaginary whip over him. "No work, no eat."

"Hey, how come that's the first Bible verse you memorized?" Ken asked, cowering in mock fear.

"That's in the Bible?"

"It sure is."

"Oh. It's what Dad used to say when Saturday chores got sluffed." She grinned at him. "So, obey the Bible and help."

"I can't cook."

Stacey noted his crossed fingers and laughed. "I'm sure you can make toast." She led them to the kitchen, giving directions as she went. "Ken, the toaster's in that corner cupboard, top shelf of the lazy susan. The bread's in the pantry over there. And here's the butter."

Erica laughed. "And what do I do?"

"You can clean lettuce, set the table, put some chips in a bowl—Ken, get the potato chips out when you get the bread—and I guess that's all. Mike, you can slice tomatoes and help Erica."

"What does that leave for you?" protested Ken. "You can't just be supervisor."

"I don't intend to. Someone with enormous cooking skill has to do the bacon. That's my job."

With a lot of laughter and sly, knowing questions from the guys, they put together a mountain of sandwiches. They devoured the lot, along with potato chips, carrot and celery sticks, pickles and olives. When the table was empty, Stacey offered, "There's ice cream."

Ken groaned. "Maybe later. Right now, I'm stuffed."

"Me, too," chorused Mike and Erica.

"Well, that took an hour or so," Ken said. "What do we do next?"

"Clean up after ourselves," said Stacey. "That means dishes."

They were about finished when Ken asked, "Has anything more happened with our mystery?"

Stacey took one last wipe at the sink, hung the dishcloth over the divider, and turned to lean against the counter. "Yes. Quite a bit. Come into the living room, and I'll fill you in."

Mike and Erica sat together on the couch. Stacey and

Ken chose adjoining easy chairs. "First," asked Stacey, "did you follow me home last night?"

"No." Mike looked at Ken. "He wanted me to, but you had said you'd be all right. What happened?"

"Nothing. Well, not on the way home. Mom got a strange phone call. Someone said they knew where I was and where Dad was. She panicked and called those two CIA agents. They said they'd send agent Dicks to follow me and make sure I got home all right. I just didn't know for sure who was behind me."

"Scared?" asked Erica.

"Not really. They didn't push or get too close. All that was last night. This morning the agents came over. They were a little upset that I'd told you about the case—particularly the older one, agent Riley. He's the one in charge. He even thought you might have made the call to Mom."

"Did you think we did?" Mike asked.

"Of course not." Stacey grinned. "Even if the thought had crossed my mind, it couldn't have been you. I was with you when the call was made."

"Did the agents chew you out?"

"No. But while they were here, Mom got another phone call. A threatening one." Stacey told them all that had happened that morning, then about the call offering her the job, and Colin's abrupt change of attitude toward her when she'd mentioned Neva Boyce.

They talked about their mystery for a couple of hours, suggesting everything from logical reasons to wild ideas.

Ken wound up the evening. "I don't think we're getting anywhere," he said with a laugh. "We really haven't come up with much. Besides, Stacey and I have a date for five-thirty tomorrow morning to go bird watching and I've got to get some sleep. Let's pray together before we go."

The four stood in a circle and clasped hands. Ken prayed, "Thank you, Father, for providing an evening more fun and interesting than anything we could think up. We pray your continued protection for Stacey and her family.

We ask in Jesus' name, Amen."

Ken lingered a moment on the doorstep as Mike and Erica dashed to the car. "I know God will watch over you. I'll see you in the morning."

"Five-thirty sharp."

"Right." A warm touch to her shoulder, then he was gone.

When he pulled up in front of the house in the morning, Stacey let herself out quietly. Her binoculars dangled around her neck, her pockets bulged with dried bread and snacks, and she held her bird book.

"Good morning," she greeted him, slipping into the front seat beside him. "Mom just got home an hour or so ago, and I didn't want to wake her."

"Does she know you're going?"

"Yes. She said I could bring you back for breakfast if I liked."

"And?"

"We'll see how quiet you are in the woods," she teased. "If you don't scare the birds away, I'll consider it."

"The most noise I'll make will be the infinitesimal click of the shutter."

When they arrived at the woods, Ken parked along the dead-end road and lifted his gear out of the trunk. "Here," he said, "you're not carrying much. You can take the camera bag while I get the rest."

"What do you do when you're all alone?"

"Leave some of it home."

They started down the trail. "Where to?" asked Stacey softly. "What would you like to photograph this morning?"

"Whatever bird you've been trying to spot and I've ruined for you."

Stacey laughed. "Then it's to a place that has both big trees and brush. Almost any place in these woods."

They soon found a spot. "Do you want to hide under a

cedar tree?'' he whispered. "I can't—have to have the camera out in the open."

"It's okay. I like the cedars because it gives me a little freedom of movement." Stacey chuckled. "I can scratch my nose or move a cone without scaring the birds. But as long as we're still, they'll come."

Ken set up his camera on a low tripod, while Stacey scattered dry bread crumbs around the area. She sat down Indian-style next to Ken and his tripod.

"Oooh. It's drier under the cedar trees." Her voice was a mere whisper of sound.

"Have just the thing," Ken mouthed, digging into his oversized case. He pulled out two thin, plastic-covered pillows and handed her one.

She scooted it under her. "Much better."

They settled down in companionable silence to await the coming of whatever wildlife might appear. Birds twittered, and rustlings in the underbrush indicated small animals starting their new day.

Stacey felt constrained, knowing that movements normally hidden by her guardian cedars would now scare the wildlife. From time to time, Ken tested the light and readjusted his lens. His movements, slow and relaxed, didn't startle the robins, varied thrushes or juncos that had found the bread crumbs. They kept hopping, scratching, and eating. Once in a while one would cock a beady black eye at them, but after a thorough scrutiny, would go back to its morning task.

Stacey wiggled a finger to attract Ken's attention. Mimicking his slow, easy movements, she pointed to a small, gray rabbit munching on wild carrot.

He swung the camera, focused, and snapped the bunny just as it turned to face them full on, one ear cocked, the other drooping. Ken smiled down at her. "Good shot," he mouthed.

He snapped a brown creeper circling its way up an alder tree, a nuthatch making its way headfirst down an old maple.

A porcupine, quills tucked safely away, passed so close he almost brushed the leg of the tripod. He gave them a wary glance and lumbered on his way.

Stacey was about to give up, when Ken waggled a finger at her. She followed the slight nod of his head. A small bush moved across an open space.

Ken snapped shot after shot as the bush skittered along. Stacey put a hand to her mouth to silence the giggle that threatened to burst out. The expression on Ken's face was a cross between bewilderment and excitement.

When the apparition finally passed out of sight, Stacey lay back on the ground and hooted with laughter. "You— you looked so funny! But you kept on taking pictures!"

"I couldn't miss capturing that on film. At first I thought it was a walking bush like in the Tolkien trilogy. What was it?" he asked. "Some little creature playing camouflage war games?"

Stacey gasped and chuckled again before she could answer. "It's what folks around here call a mountain or meadow beaver. He'd chewed off a branch and was taking it home for breakfast."

Ken grinned down at her. "When I first saw it, I couldn't believe my eyes. He finally got to an angle where I could see him and not just the bush."

"I wish I'd had a camera to take a picture of you. But, I admit I felt much the same the first time I saw it. One doesn't expect a leafy plant to go cross-country."

"And you know what you've done?" he asked in mock sternness. "*You're* the one who made the noise and scared all the wildlife away!"

"It was worth it. Besides, it's about time to head home for Mom's fluffy cheese souffle served up with hot biscuits and honey."

"Are you including me at that table?"

Stacey cocked her head as if considering. "Well, you were quiet this morning. I guess I have to keep my word." Her face became serious. "Besides, I'd like you to meet my mom. I feel like I'm just getting to know her and she's rather a nice person.''

The next afternoon, Stacey sprawled across her bed waiting for Becky. She'd read everything Becky had suggested, and she was ready to ask some questions with her notebook and Bible handy.

Her thoughts drifted back to the day before. The breakfast with Ken and her mom had been great. Her mom had taken to Ken immediately, and Ken was both friendly and respectful. They'd laughed and joked, touched a little on the mystery, but mostly just talked and ate.

This morning Ken had been waiting in the church foyer for her. She'd felt so warm and accepted. Mike and Erica joined them, and they all sat together during the service. But the concepts in the sermon were so new and challenging, Stacey soon forgot everything else. She took notes and nodded gratefully to Ken when he helped her find verses in her Bible.

Dragging her thoughts back to the present, Stacey reviewed the verse she'd memorized, then glanced around her room. It looked so different from last week. She hoped Becky would notice. And then, Becky was there.

"Hi. Your mom said to come on up. May I come in?"

Stacey rolled off the bed. "Of course. Take the easy chair."

Becky dumped an armload of books on the dresser and looked around. "What a difference! You've really made a drastic change in a hurry. I'm proud of you."

"Well, it doesn't look this good all the time, but I'm improving."

"And that is what God expects of us. To give it our best and when we fail, to confess it to Him and start over."

They talked for a few minutes about the events of the week, then Becky said, "Tell me about your date with Charlie."

"I recognized before we left the house that all he wanted

was to use me to discover information about Dad. I think he still believed we had a direct line to him or something. Anyway, I didn't give him any significant information."

Stacey cocked her head to one side. "You weren't very pleased that I was going out with Charlie. Why didn't you want me to date him?"

"I guess I overreacted—taking my job of discipling you too seriously. I've never discipled anyone before."

"That's all right. I want to learn all I can. Tell me— why shouldn't I go out with him?"

"My first reaction wasn't because of Charlie at all. It was that you were breaking a commitment to Erica. That's part of what I'd like us to talk about today. But there is something else. A Christian really shouldn't date a non-Christian. The Bible tells us we shouldn't be in close relationship with unbelievers."

"But you always spent time with me, took me places," Stacey protested. "I wasn't a Christian then."

"I'm not saying we're supposed to avoid non-Christians. How would we ever win them to Christ? But we're not supposed to get into relationships where we're bound to non-Christians—like marriage, business partners, that kind of relationship."

"I see. If I were to date Charlie seriously, my relationship with him might make me lose my interest in being a Christian."

"Or at least draw you away from the things God wants you to think about and do."

"Well, I don't have to worry about this guy. There's absolutely no attraction between us. Not only was he just prying for information, our likes and dislikes are poles apart."

"Good. I'd been praying this week that you wouldn't get involved with him." Becky reached for her books. "Ready to start?"

"Yes. I have a few questions for you."

The girls spent the next hour going over Stacey's questions, reviewing the memory verse, and discussing the booklet on assurance.

When they'd finished, Becky asked, "How would you like to do a Bible study with just the two of us? I borrowed a book from Dondra that the high school class is going through, thinking it would be just the thing to help you set up your quiet time and get off to a good start."

She showed Stacey a book called *Building Christian Discipline*. "It sounds sort of tough, but look . . ." Becky flipped to the first section. "Here's several lessons telling how to have a quiet time, with suggestions to keep it interesting and exciting."

Stacey took the book and leafed through the pages. Becky leaned over her shoulder. "Look, here's a lesson on commitment. That's the one that caught my eye. If you'd like, we can get copies and go through the whole thing or just the lessons that look like they meet a need we both have."

"I'm game," Stacey said. "I'm beginning to realize how much I have to learn. I'll pick up a copy this week."

"Me, too. Do you want to start at the beginning and work through?"

"Let's do the lesson on commitment first. Then go back to the beginning. Okay?"

They made a list of things to pray about and spent a few minutes praying together.

When they finished, Stacey said, "Mom is making stroganoff sandwiches. They're delicious. Can you stay and eat with us before we go on to church?"

"I'd love to. I'll call home and let them know I won't be there for supper."

"You can use the phone in the kitchen while I help Mom. I'll tell her you'll be here for sure."

The phone rang as the girls entered the kitchen. Mrs. White reached for it. "Doug? I'm so glad to hear from you. Is everything all right? Yes, we're fine here. You will? Good."

While Mrs. White talked, Stacey finished slicing tomatoes and green peppers for the sandwiches.

Becky whispered, "What can I do?"

Stacey handed her a block of cheddar cheese and a grater. "Shred a cup of cheese. It goes on top of everything."

Much of the tension had left her mother's face when she'd finished talking. "You look five years younger, Mom," Stacey observed. "Good news from Dad?"

"Yes. He thinks he can get home next weekend. If everything goes well, they'll be at a good breaking point and he'll be able to get away."

Stacey touched her mother's arm. "Then we'll pray that the project runs like clockwork. It'll be awfully good to see Dad again. Did you tell him I got a job with his company?"

Mrs. White put her fingers across her mouth in a gesture of dismay. "I forgot."

"No problem. I'll get to tell him when he comes home."

"Oh. While you and Becky were studying, that Charlie called." Mrs. White looked a bit apprehensive. "I told him you were busy."

"I was. Did he say what he wanted?"

"No. Just that he'd call later. Caro—Stacey. You won't go out with him again? Remember your dad warned you against seeing him."

"I remember. I won't go unless you approve. If he calls, I'll find out what he wants. If we think we can get information from him, it won't hurt me to eat another good dinner."

"You'll check with me first?"

"Yes, Mom. Promise."

Chapter Eleven

Stacey remembered her promise late that night.

A prickle of apprehension looped up her back when she recognized Charlie's resonant voice on the telephone.

"Are you ready to take a chance on another dinner with me?" he asked.

"Would it be a chance?" she teased.

"Isn't any second date a c-chance?" Did he stammer a bit? "A chance that the beautiful impressions of the first date may be shattered by discovering that the prince is really a frog?"

Stacey bit back a remark that in his case it had happened on the first date.

"I've never thought of it that way. But maybe it's better to lose the illusion than to believe a fairy tale."

"Does that mean you'll go?"

"What night?"

"I was thinking of Thursday. I'm tied up until then."

"I have a commitment already for Thursday. I'm sorry."

"Then let's make it Friday. We'll go to . . . well, you can choose. I know a great restaurant that serves Japanese country-style food, or there's a terrific steak and lobster place in downtown Seattle. Which would you prefer?"

"Look, Charlie. Before I commit myself . . ." Stacey couldn't bring herself to say she had to ask her mother's permission, so she continued, "I have to check Mom's plans for that night. If things work out with her, I'd like to go. Can I call you Tuesday and let you know?"

After a long pause during which Stacey thought Charlie might have been cut off, he said, "Yes. That's okay. If you can call between one and four, I'll be at 555–3429."

"I'll be at work then, but I'm sure I can phone from there."

After Stacey hung up, she asked herself why she'd put off giving him an answer until Tuesday. Was it because she really didn't want to go, or was it to give her time to convince her mother that going would be the only way to find out what Charlie and his friends were up to?

She shrugged. Whatever it was, it was done.

She'd been preparing for bed when the call came, so she finished cleansing her face before running downstairs to talk with her mother.

Mrs. White was stretched out in an easy chair in the living room, her feet propped on the ottoman. She put down her magazine.

Stacey sank to the floor, next to her mother's knee. "That was Charlie."

"I thought so. He has a distinctive voice. Did he ask you out?"

"Yes. To dinner Friday. I told him I needed to check with you and would let him know. What do you think?"

"You know I don't want you involved with him."

"I'm not exactly eager to go, Mom. But I think it may be the only way to find out what all this is about. Charlie seems the nicest of the three. Maybe he'll let something slip, or maybe his questions will clue me in on what's happening. I think I should go."

Mrs. White wavered. Stacey saw she was about to get her way and felt a surge of anger and pity for her mother. *Why does she let me dominate her?*

"Look, Mom. Let's compromise. We'll call agent Riley

and ask his opinion. If he thinks it's at all dangerous, I'll tell Charlie no. Okay?"

Relief shone in Mrs. White's eyes. "I'll go along with that. We'll call tomorrow."

At two a.m., Stacey woke to the ringing of the telephone. She leaped to answer, hoping her mother wouldn't waken. When she said hello, there was only silence on the other end. "Hello," she repeated. "Hello?"

The line went dead.

Mrs. White peered from her bedroom door. "Who was it, Stacey?"

"No one. Probably a wrong number. They must have realized my voice wasn't the one they expected. They just hung up."

They could have at least said they were sorry, Stacey thought as she drifted back to sleep. It seemed she'd barely dropped off when the phone rang again. A glance at the clock told her it'd been an hour.

This time when she answered a whispering voice said, "Just wanted you to know you're not alone. We're watching you . . ." The line went dead.

She hung up and padded across the hall to her mother's room. Listening at the door, Stacey could hear her gentle snoring.

She went back to bed, but a niggling fear kept her from falling asleep. When the phone rang at four, she was halfway to the hall to answer before the second ring.

"What do you want?" she demanded. "Why are you calling?"

"Young girls alone shouldn't ask so many questions," the whispery voice scolded. "Just go back to bed, assured we're hovering near."

"But I'm not—" the connection broke off before Stacey could say, "alone."

Moving quietly, Stacey went from window to window peering into the first gray light that spread over the neighborhood. Nothing seemed out of place, no cars that shouldn't be there, no loitering fake workmen. Nothing. Careful not to waken her mother, she skipped the stair that creaked and went back to bed.

Her thoughts whirled. Why? Who thought she was alone? On a night when her mother worked, she could have understood, but Mom was home.

She lay awake puzzling it out when the phone rang again. She hesitated a moment. Should she answer or just let it ring? At the third ring, she crawled out of bed. She had to stop the noise.

She reached the phone at the same time her mother did. Stacey stopped the ringing by lifting the receiver. She slammed it back into its cradle—hard.

"Carol—Stacey. What—"

She was interrupted by renewed ringing.

Stacey said, "Someone's been calling every hour. They just whisper that I'm not alone, they're watching. I thought maybe the slam would discourage them."

The phone kept shrilling its summons.

"Wait a minute." Mrs. White disappeared back into her room. In a moment she returned with a whistle. "If it's the same person, maybe this will stop him."

Stacey grinned and took the whistle. She lifted the receiver, said, "Hello?"

"That wasn't very nice of you," said the whispery voice. "Not when I'm trying to help you."

"If you didn't like that," Stacey said, "what do you think about this?" She blew a shrill blast into the mouthpiece and returned the receiver to its cradle.

Too awake to even try going back to bed, Stacey and Mrs. White went down to the kitchen and made cups of hot chocolate. They sat at the table sipping the soothing drink.

"Tell me exactly what they said." Mrs. White put down her cup and drew her robe more closely around her. "Everything."

"The first time nothing was said, they just hung up. I thought it was a wrong number. The next two times, they whispered something about my not being alone, that they were watching me."

"Why would anyone think you were alone? My car's in the driveway. Anyone who knows us would realize I'm here, not at work."

"I know. It doesn't make sense. What . . ." Stacey snapped her fingers. "I've got it. I bet I know."

"What?"

"When I told Charlie I couldn't give him an answer until Tuesday—that I had to talk to you first, I'll wager today's salary he thought you were gone or working or something."

"So it's all part of the same thing. Do you see why I don't want you to go with him?"

"Of course, Mom, but don't you see that going with him may be the only way to stop all this? If agent Riley agrees, I want more than ever to see Charlie Friday night."

Mrs. White nodded wearily. "If agent Riley agrees. I don't suppose they'll call again now that it's daylight. I think I'll try to get some sleep."

"I may as well shower and get ready for work."

Stacey almost forgot how tired she was as she started her new job. Her suspicion that the job was just a "gimme" because her dad worked for them disappeared when she realized they had a lot of work for her and expected her to do it quickly and well.

Because it related to her interest field, she found even the repetitive task of entering data exciting and informative. She even remembered to breath a quick thank you to God for providing a job that would enhance her learning and better prepare her for college in the fall.

Colin Trent was polite but distant as he showed her what was expected of her and taught her the procedure for entering data on the computer. He didn't renew his invitation for lunch, but at noon he conducted her to the cafeteria and included her in a group around one of the tables.

"How's the first day going?"

"Like the work so far?"

"Think you're going to enjoy it here?"

At first, Stacey was a little reserved as she parried their questions, thinking Colin may have influenced them against her. But they seemed genuinely interested, and soon she relaxed and responded with enthusiasm. *Whatever Colin suspects about me*, she thought, *he must not have passed it on to anyone else.*

After lunch, Colin left her at the computer terminal with a stack of records to be entered. "You probably won't finish these by five," he stated. "If you do, my extension is 3146. Oh, you get a break about three. If I don't get back for you, go on down to the cafeteria."

Stacey wrinkled her nose at his back as he walked out of the room. "You probably won't finish these by five," she mimicked under her breath. "I'll show you, Colin Trent."

She grabbed the first sheet and attacked the keyboard with a vengeance. An hour later, she leaned back in the chair and stretched her back. She'd made a small dent in the pile, but Colin was probably right. She wouldn't finish by five. She probably wouldn't finish by five tomorrow.

Flexing her fingers, she picked up the next sheet and started again. A couple of workers paused just outside the door. Their voices drifted in.

"I can't believe it. We're not working on anything that highly classified."

Stacey ignored them and took the next record.

"Believe it. Doug White is."

Her fingers stilled at the mention of her father's name. Her fingers quiet on the keyboard, her eyes on the screen, she tuned out the record in front of her and listened.

"But he's on loan. Not even here."

"True, but this is his home base. And if what the boss told us a couple of weeks ago, that woman who tried to force her way in here with false credentials—"

"Neva Boyce. I'll bet she was mad when they exposed her."

"Probably more scared than mad. I'm sure she was assigned to discover what White is working on and nab it. Failure in a mission like that can mean death in an operation like hers."

The other voice laughed. "Oh, come on. You've been reading too many spy novels. She's probably just industrial espionage."

"Yeah? What industry is working on—"

"Shut it. You know better than to . . ."

A sudden silence in the hall made Stacey feel like a butterfly about to be pinned to a board. She made her fingers fly over the keys as if she were oblivious to everything but the work in front of her.

She thought she heard, "White's daughter," as the voices faded down the hall. So, that's what this is all about— Dad's secret project. The staff has been warned that Neva Boyce is a spy.

No wonder Colin had turned off. No wonder they were so desperate to find her father. Her fingers stopped. It still didn't make sense. Her father was in Denver, at the lab there. It should have been no problem finding him. Was all that just a ruse? Something to keep any suspicious officials busy here while they stole the project in Denver?

Stacey shook her head. She kept getting more and more pieces to the puzzle, but they didn't fit together.

She sensed someone behind her and turned.

"Ah, now. Stacey. How's the work going?"

"Fine, sir." Her chaotic thoughts disappeared as she again concealed a smile at the director's wild-scientist look. "I'm making headway with this stack of records."

"Good. Good. Are you learning anything?"

"Yes." *More than you bargained for*, she thought silently. "I already love the job. Thanks for calling me."

"Just keep at it. You'll do fine." He picked up a folder from a nearby file and left.

By five, only a two-inch stack of records was left to be entered. Colin came in to show her where to file the completed ones and where to store those yet to be done. He unbent a little, seeing how much she'd accomplished.

"You really tore into those, didn't you?" he said. "I didn't expect you to even get half of them done today."

She tried out a smile on him. "I like a challenge. I was hoping to get them all done."

He smiled back. "To make me eat crow?"

"Well, yes. If your goal was to make me work hard, you succeeded. Or maybe you were just testing my loyalty?"

His smile disappeared and the hard look came back to his eyes.

Why did I remind him? Stacey scolded herself. *He was just becoming human again.* "I'm off," she went on, trying not to notice his coldness. "See you in the morning."

He only nodded and preceded her out the door, disappearing down the hall at a half-run.

When Stacey let herself into the house forty-five minutes later, her mother, agents Riley and Dicks, and a woman she'd never seen before were drinking coffee around the kitchen table.

"How was your first day at work?" Agent Dicks grinned at her. "Keep you hopping?"

"No. Sitting." Stacey leaned against the counter and smiled back at him. "I've been entering data on a computer all afternoon. Are my shoulders stiff!"

"Sit here, and I'll give you a massage," her mother said, rising from her chair.

"Later, Mom. Enjoy your coffee." She looked from one face to another. "Isn't anyone going to introduce me?"

"You mean you don't know your Aunt Miriam?" Agent Dicks asked.

"I don't have an Aunt Miriam."

"Of course you do," Riley entered the conversation. "Your mother's younger sister. She's come to visit for a spell."

"Probably quite a spell from the amount of luggage deposited in the front hall." Dicks' eyes brimmed with laughter. "A trunk, two large suitcases, plus some small bags."

The woman smiled at Stacey. "I'm Miriam Parker, a co-agent with these two. When Riley called here this morning and heard about your hassling phone calls through the night, we decided it was time to bring me in."

"Is it necessary?" Stacey asked. "Oh, not that we mind having you here, but no threats have been made. Just nuisance calls."

"Remember Grandma's slogan," Dicks said. "Better safe than sorry. If this group hasn't found what they wanted, they may be getting desperate."

"We don't want to take any chances with you or your mother," added Riley. "Everyone else in your family has more protection than you and you're the focus of the attack. Mrs. Parker stays."

"Won't they know Mom doesn't have a sister named Miriam? Won't that make them think we're being devious for some reason?"

Riley scratched his chin, nodding. "You're right. Miriam, could you be a college classmate?"

"Make it high school. Our college majors are too far apart for us to have become friends there." She paused for a moment, a thoughtful expression on her lined face. "Yes, that should do it. We've kept in touch all these years, and I finally made it to this part of the country."

"Better decide which high school and where," suggested Dicks. "You don't want to be unable to answer questions. That's worse than out and out admitting you're an agent."

Miriam Parker glared at him. "I've been an agent longer than you have, Richard, my boy. I don't need a review on basics."

"Yes, ma'am," he said meekly.

"Mom, did you ask them about Friday night?"

"We talked about it."

Stacey refilled their coffee cups. "And?"

"We've decided to let you go," said agent Riley. "Provided you follow a few simple rules."

"Of course. What are they?"

"We know in advance where you're going, you go there, and then make some excuse to come right home. We don't want to risk losing you in traffic following you from place to place."

Stacey swallowed rising pride. "That's easy enough. Charlie offered me my choice of a Japanese restaurant or a steak and lobster place—both in downtown Seattle. I'll opt for the steak and lobster. . . ."

Riley scribbled the name she mentioned in a notebook. "Agent Dicks will be there, too. What time does Charlie pick you up?"

"Seven-thirty."

"Okay. Dicks will manage to be seated after you. We'll arrange to give him a table where he can keep an eye on you, but not too close. Don't recognize him or let on you're aware he's there," instructed Riley.

"If they're watching the house, they'll recognize him."

"Possibly, but we don't think they're watching the house, just listening. So please, don't let on you know him."

"Unless you're in trouble," Dicks put in. "Then come after Richard, and I'll take you home. Got it?"

Stacey grinned at him. "Got it, Uncle. I choose the steak and lobster, I see you, but don't recognize you. When dinner's over, I come right home because I've had a hard week at work or Mom's friend is here or I have a headache."

"Right on."

The next couple of days moved rapidly. Tuesday, Stacey called Charlie during her afternoon break and told him she'd be able to go Friday night. "Mom's old high school friend popped into town," she explained. "We decided it would be okay for me to take time out for dinner. They're so busy talking about the olden days, they probably won't even miss me."

She enjoyed her work, glad for some variety. Fortunately, she hadn't had to spend more than an hour or two on the computer since Monday afternoon. She kept busy running errands, filing, and a host of small jobs the scientists were delighted to push off on her.

Even Colin was lightening up again. Perhaps he didn't think she was a traitor after all. Or he'd decided that being with her was the way to discover if he were right or wrong. Stacey grimaced. Maybe he'd been given instructions to keep an eye on her.

Thursday morning, he renewed his invitation for lunch. "Hey. You promised we'd have lunch one day this week. How about today?"

"We've had lunch together the last three days," she reminded him.

"But not alone. Let's skip the cafeteria and go out where we can get acquainted. Who knows? You might even decide we could have dinner one night."

Stacey laughed. "That's pushing it, but we'll give it a try."

Their camaraderie continued through lunch. They discovered they liked the same music, the same foods, even some of the same movies. Hurrying back to the office, Colin said, "How about it? Do I get to take you to dinner tomorrow night?"

"No." Stacey laughed. "Only because I already have a date for tomorrow night."

"How about Saturday then?"

"That would work out. At what time?"

"I'll pick you up at seven."

They were within a half-block of the lab, when a woman bumped into Stacey.

"Oh, sorry, Stacey! I thought you'd forgotten we were to meet today. I'd given up on you."

Stacey could hardly believe her eyes. There stood Neva Boyce, talking as if she were a long lost friend. Stacey stared at her, totally confused. "I didn't—"

"Oh, that's okay. How could an old friend compete with

a young man for your attention?" Her mauve lips smiled an oily smile. "But I do need to see you, you know. We have some things we just have to discuss."

"I don't—"

"I know. You don't have time now. Maybe we can get together this weekend to make up for this missed appointing." Shifting her handbag to the other shoulder, the black-haired woman turned and sauntered down the sidewalk.

Stacey stared after her, then looked up at Colin. "I never said I'd meet her. You've got to believe I have nothing to do with her."

"If you say so. Who is she?"

"You don't know? You've been withdrawn and unfriendly most of the week because I asked about her, and you don't even know what Neva Boyce looks like?"

"Neva Boyce? The spy?"

Chapter Twelve

Later that night, after another lesson on the Song of Solomon, Stacey squeezed into the booth at the Shanty with Ken, Mike, Erica, and Becky. The addition of Erica's brother, Alex, and his friend, Harry, made a tight fit.

The Shanty had added a couple of new specialties, and soon a waitress plopped a heaping platter of potato skins in the middle of the table followed by a large plate of nachos. She returned with their sodas and small plates for everyone.

"Dig in," Ken invited. "There's enough here for a small army."

"Which we seem to be." Erica flexed her elbows. "We're going to have to find a bigger booth if we keep growing."

"Good. The more the merrier." Mike smiled at the younger boys. "How was your meeting tonight?"

"Okay," Alex said, popping a dripping-with-cheese nacho into his mouth.

Harry, his mouth already crammed with potato skins, only nodded.

"Can I ask a question?" Stacey reached for a nacho. "In tonight's lesson, Ken, you were talking about the different names of God. You mentioned His being our Lord or Master, but you stressed His being Father. Is there really a difference?"

"Definitely," Ken answered. "If He were just Lord or Master, we would be only slaves."

"But we are." Stacey pulled out her New Testament and turned to Romans 6. "This is one of the verses I found that made me become a Christian." She read the verse about being slaves to whichever master you choose.

"That's right, but it's not the whole picture, only one piece—like a piece of a jigsaw puzzle. Look up . . . let's see." He leafed through the pages of his New Testament. "Check Romans 8 . . . just a few pages farther. It says we received a Spirit of sonship, making us children of God and co-heirs with Christ."

"Look at 1 John 3:1," Becky urged. "It tells us that because of God's lavish love, he calls us His children. Children that will one day be just like Christ."

"So, we are slaves—" Stacey began.

"Yes. Since He bought us and owns us." Becky flipped through her Bible. "That's found in 1 Corinthians 6 and 7."

"And I just read much the same thing this morning in the first chapter of 1 Peter," Erica chimed in.

"But," Ken continued, "we're more than slaves. Christ elevated us to being His children because of His love for us."

Alex waited for a pause in the conversation and turned to Stacey. "I'm not trying to change the subject, but I've heard rumors of a mystery. Will you tell me about it?"

Stacey hesitated. Should she tell anyone else? She couldn't resist the appeal in his eyes. Besides, wasn't he the one most responsible for solving the Tyson case? Maybe he'd be a help. "Why not? I hear you're a good mystery buff."

Stacey briefly outlined what had happened. She suppressed a smile as both Harry and Alex took notes in grubby notebooks with stubby pencils.

She finished by telling of Miriam, the CIA agent, who had moved in with them and said, "Oh. I have another date with Charlie tomorrow night."

"Is that safe?" Becky asked.

Erica added, "Are you sure it's the right thing to do?"

Stacey shrugged. "It's all settled. Mom and I discussed it, then we asked the agents if it would be all right. They agreed. Agent Dicks will be there to keep an eye on me."

"Good." Ken rested a hand on her shoulder. "That makes me feel better."

Mike rubbed his knuckles against each other. "But what do you hope to find out?"

"What this is all about. I overheard a conversation at work. They think Neva Boyce is a spy. If she is, then it stands to reason both Arnold Tenley and Charlie are spies, too."

"Obvious deduction," Harry muttered.

"It's just that they're doing strange things—like hanging around here when Dad and the project he's involved with are in Colorado. They've got the CIA stumped. They're not pursuing things as they would if they're really after whatever it is Dad's working on."

"Does your Dad know all this?" Alex asked.

"Yes. We talk to him almost every day to check up on each other."

Alex persisted. "Does he do anything other than be a scientist?"

"No. Well, what do you mean?"

"Well, you said the project he's working on is government and it's top secret. Does he do other things for the government—like, is he a spy himself?"

"Dad? Never. He's not the adventurous type, except when it comes to new discoveries in science." Stacey grinned. "My dad a spy? I can't imagine it."

"Just asking. This all might make some sense if he were."

They rehashed some of the events, but made no headway. Finally, Erica said, "Well, it's time we got home. There's work tomorrow."

On the drive home, Ken said, "I wish my schedule were

more predictable. I wanted to take you to a concert tomorrow night, but I didn't know until this afternoon if I'd have the time off. The concert's repeated on Saturday. If I can get the tickets switched, will you go?"

Stacey's heart sank. Why had she said yes to Colin's dinner invitation? Was she wishy-washy? Could she call Colin and cancel? Remembering the verse she was memorizing with Becky, "who keeps his oath even when it hurts," she sighed. This hurt, but she'd keep her word.

"I'm sorry, Ken." Stacey reached out to touch his arm. He captured her hand with his. "I have a date for Saturday night."

Colin had acted as if he wasn't quite ready to believe she hadn't had an appointment with Neva Boyce. His friendliness had taken a freezer dip again, but he hadn't said anything about canceling the date.

Ken turned to smile at her. "My bad luck. Surely you haven't committed Saturday morning away already?"

"No. Do you want to try for my mini's again?"

"Or mountain beavers or whatever other wildlife may come creeping through the trees."

They laughed, remembering the meandering bush of last Saturday morning.

The next day flew by. Stacey stood in front of her mirror adding a last touch of lipstick. Charlie would be here in a few minutes and an anticipatory tingle zipped up and down her spine. Would she discover anything tonight?

She took several deep breaths to appear calm and unconcerned in front of her mother. In the kitchen, Mrs. White and Miriam lingered over apple crisp and steaming coffee.

Stacey whirled around. "How do I look?"

"You're beautiful, my dear," Miriam said, a twinkle in her eye. "Much too beautiful for the caliber of your date."

Stacey flashed a warning glance at her, but asked in a lighthearted voice, "Have you convinced Mom I'm going to be perfectly safe with agent Dicks guarding me?"

The two older women exchanged glances.

"Probably not," Miriam said, "but she's willing to go along with us." Her voice grew more serious. "But—you be careful. Don't do or say anything to antagonize this guy. More importantly, don't go off on your own. Those are strict orders. Do you understand?"

Stacey squashed rising resentment and said, "Yes'm. I know what I'm supposed to do and not do." She couldn't keep all the snap from her voice.

"Stacey," Mrs. White pleaded. "It's for your own safety."

"I know, Mom. I'll do exactly what they say. Promise." The doorbell chimed a summons. "And there's Charlie. I'll see you later, probably around eleven."

Charlie helped her with her coat and tenderly ushered her into the car. "Where to?"

"I've chosen the steak and lobster. Japanese was hard to resist, but I haven't had a good lobster dinner in ages."

"Then Brownings, here we come. Me and the loveliest gal in town."

"Flattery, Mr. Place? Surely you know many women much more lovely and sophisticated than I."

He looked at her and smiled. "Sophisticated, yes. Lovelier? No. And you've grown more so since we first met. There's something about your eyes that glows. I'm not sure what it is. But it's different, and I like it."

More flattery. I wonder what he's up to tonight, mused Stacey before replying.

"Thank you. Maybe I'll tell you what I think it is one of these days."

"Tonight?"

"Maybe."

Charlie kept the conversation light and frothy as he threaded through the evening traffic into Seattle. At Brownings, they were shown to a partially secluded table. Both slid into an upholstered wicker seat that backed to a row of lighted stained glass windows.

"Excuse me just a moment," Charlie said. "I made reservations at both places. I'll just call and cancel the other. Must keep in good with the head waiters."

Stacey liked the immaculate white tablecloth which made an elegant background for black and silver plates. A single pink rose in a crystal vase managed to purvey its fragrance above the other scents in the room.

"You do know the nice places to eat," Stacey said when Charlie returned. "I hope the food is as good as the atmosphere."

"Better. Wait until you taste the lobster. It's fresh and perfectly served."

"Sounds good." She picked up the menu and glanced at the offered fare. "In fact, I'll skip the steak and have just lobster."

Charlie ordered lobster for both and twisted in the seat to face her. He reached for her hand.

"Now, tell me. Where do you get the glow?"

"You really want to know?" Stacey stalled for time. Could she tell this man, who she thought was a spy, about Jesus? She could and she would. A slight tremor shook her voice as she started. "About the time—in fact, the very day we met, I met someone else."

"Another guy? I should have known. You've fallen in love. Then why are you out with me?"

"Fallen in love? Yes, you could say that. But not just another guy. I met Jesus, God's Son. In just this short time, two weeks exactly, He's made some tremendous changes in me."

"Like what?"

"Well, He's taken away some resentments and bitterness. He's teaching me commitment and submission. Because of His Spirit in my life, I have a better relationship with my mother than ever before."

"That's a lot for two weeks. What did you do?"

"Just accepted that He died for me. Asked Him to forgive my sins."

"You're too young to have done much sinning."

Stacey looked wistfully across the room, saw agent Dicks walk in with a striking redhead. She brought her attention back to Charlie. "I wish that were true. I've done some really bad things, but I'm finding God forgives anything."

Charlie had been watching as agent Dicks and the redhead were seated at a table across the way. He nodded toward them. "Know that couple?"

Stacey held her breath as she made a pretense of following his gesture. "Oh, she's beautiful, isn't she? No. I've never seen her before."

If Charlie noticed that she hadn't referred to agent Dicks, he made no mention of it. Their salads were served, and the conversation turned to the food, the weather, and Stacey's new job.

Over dessert, Stacey told Charlie that she'd run into Neva on Thursday, but didn't tell him what Neva had said. She wasn't sure if that was what made him nervous or if it were only the passing of time, but he glanced at his watch every few seconds. His eyes kept roaming over the patrons at nearby tables.

Stacey followed his gaze, but saw no one familiar except agent Dicks, who appeared totally unaware of her and her companion.

After the umpteenth time he'd checked his watch, she laid her hand on his arm. "If you have another date, or you're in a hurry, I'm ready. I don't need to finish this coffee."

He looked down at her hand, then covered it with his. When his glance met hers, his eyes were bleak and his face looked grim.

She smiled. "It's okay. Let's go."

"No. You don't understand. I . . . ." His look seemed to plead with her, then she saw something change. He'd hardened, like he had just made a decision. "Come on. We're getting out of here."

Charlie threw a fifty-dollar bill on the table and grabbed her arm, lifting her from the seat. He put his hand at her back and guided her through the restaurant away from the entrance.

Stacey cast a backward glance toward agent Dicks. Did he notice?

His eyes briefly met hers, then he turned away. Wasn't he going to do anything? She couldn't resist without making a big scene, and she hesitated to do that.

"Hurry." Charlie rushed her past other diners, a serving station and through the hallway that led to the restrooms.

For a moment an hysterical giggle threatened to burst from Stacey. Was he going to take her through the restroom and out a window like the private eye TV programs? Didn't he know most restrooms didn't even have windows?

But Charlie opened a door marked private and urged her into a storage area. On the far side of the room, an exit door opened and Charlie guided her into the balmy night air.

"Aren't we—" Stacey started.

"No. We'll find a taxi. Come on."

They rounded the corner of the building and stopped short. A big black car blocked the alley. The glow from a street light gleamed off Arnold Tenley's bald head as he leaned against the car. He pushed away from the front fender.

"I thought you might get cold feet. Figured you were soft on the girl."

Charlie's arm, which had been propelling Stacey forward, now drew her slightly behind him. "You've got it all wrong, Arnie. Just adding a little flavor, a bit of romance to the evening."

Stacey's eyes widened as a small snub-nosed revolver appeared in Tenley's hand. "Sure," he sneered. "Well, I'll add some romance, too. Get in the car. Both of you."

"Stacey?" The voice preceded footsteps from the alleyway behind them. "Stacey?"

Fury flattened Tenley's already pug face. The gun disappeared from his fist and he dived into the car. It backed with a roar down the alley just as agent Dicks rounded the corner.

He looked from Charlie to Stacey and back again. "I think maybe I'd better see the young lady home. Back alley rendezvous are a bit out of her line."

"Who are you?" Charlie demanded. "I'll see she gets safely home."

"Just say I'm standing in as her big brother." Agent Dicks took Stacey's arm. "Thank him nicely for the dinner, Stacey. Then let's get out of here."

Stacey glared at him. He didn't have to treat her like a ten-year-old. For a moment, rebellious words tumbled to get out, to tell him she'd go home with whomever she pleased, but some prompting inside held them back.

She stared eye to eye with agent Dicks while she fought her inner battle. Finally she shrugged and turned to Charlie. Laying her hand on his arm, she said, "I really did enjoy the dinner. And thanks. I'm sure you were trying to—"

"Don't." Charlie covered her hand with his for a moment. "I wouldn't have made it. You're safe due to your big brother here. Watch yourself, and don't go anywhere alone." His grasp on her hand tightened. "Thanks for telling me about that glow. I wish I'd heard about it sooner."

"It's not too late. Here." Stacey opened her clutch bag and pulled out the New Testament. "I learned all about it in here. Take it."

He looked deeply into her eyes, then flipped her chin with a gentle forefinger. His gaze shifted to agent Dicks. "Take care of her."

"I think perhaps you ought to come with me."

"No way." And Charlie was off, running through the alley, cutting between two buildings.

Stacey sensed agent Dicks straining to follow him, but held back because he was committed to keeping her safe.

He put his arm across her shoulders and walked her back

to the restaurant. "Come on. I'll pay my bill, then take you home."

As they neared the house, Stacey broke a long silence. "They were going to kidnap me, weren't they?"

"That's what it looked like."

"Charlie was trying to get me away before they did."

"At the last minute. His job was probably to leave the restaurant at the exact moment when someone waiting in front could grab you."

"But he didn't."

"No. For some reason he backed out. It's apt to cost him."

Stacey stared across the dark car at the agent. "His job?"

"Maybe more. No gang will ever use him again. They know he can't be trusted." Agent Dicks turned to her with a grim smile. "Am I glad we decided to go with you tonight."

"Me, too." Tremors made her weak as the realization of what could have happened sank in. She straightened. "But, we don't have to tell Mother, do we? She'd panic."

"I'm afraid we do. There's no way not to, even if I didn't think it was best. Charlie isn't bringing you home. I am."

"You could just drop me off at the door. Mom wouldn't know it wasn't Charlie. Look," she pleaded. "It'll just worry Mom. I won't get to go anywhere until you find a way to put these guys away. At the rate you're going, that could be the rest of my adult life."

"And if we don't tell, the rest of your adult life could be a matter of days. Sorry, Stacey. Your safety comes first." He pulled to the curb in front of the White house and turned to her. "We're really not so slow. Things could break any day. In fact, this attempt tonight may be what we needed."

"How? You didn't catch them."

"We got a license number."

"But we already know who they are. If all you need is a name, you have it. What good would a plate number be?"

"Just leave the sleuthing to the CIA. Now, let's take you in."

Mrs. White and Miriam looked up from an angular design of dominoes spread across the dining room table.

"Who's winning?" Stacey asked.

"I'm afraid your mother's whipping me," Miriam said, then went right on without a pause, "Richard, you took the girl away from her date?"

"He had plans not conducive to her welfare."

Color drained from Mrs. White's already pale face. "What happened?"

"Nothing, Mom. At the last minute, Charlie tried to back out, to get me away from the rest of the gang. He almost made it, too. Then," and Stacey made a face at agent Dicks, "my knight in tweed armor came to my rescue. All's well."

"Closer watch?" asked Miriam.

Agent Dicks nodded. "Definitely."

"You mean you're going to tail me wherever I go?" demanded Stacey.

"Worse," Miriam smiled. "We're going with you. To work, to play, to . . ."

"To church and the youth meeting?"

"Right."

Stacey grinned. "Bodyguards at church." Her smile faded. "How about dates?"

"Even dates. Do you have one coming up?"

"Tomorrow night with Colin Trent from the lab. We're just going to dinner. He's got to be all right. He has a classified rating and all that clearance."

"We're not worried about your dates and friends. We're worried about Charlie or his cohorts showing up and carrying you off somewhere where we can't find you."

Mrs. White turned a domino over and over. "You're sure they'll try again?"

"No. But we won't take a chance. Understand, Stacey?"

"Yeah. Don't worry, Mom. I'll be all right. I think I'll

go up to bed now." She walked to the door, then turned. "Thanks, Richard, for intervening and bringing me home. I—oh, your date. That beautiful redhead. What—"

"You drew Alycia?" Miriam asked. "You're far luckier than you deserve."

Stacey looked from one to the other.

"Alycia is another agent," agent Dicks explained. "She tailed the car that roared out of the alley. I'll meet her soon and see what happened."

Chapter Thirteen

Stacey's alarm rang at five. Instantly awake, she shut it off and slid out of bed and noiselessly slipped into her clothes.

She hadn't mentioned her bird watching date with Ken last night—now she was glad. She wanted this one last bit of freedom before the CIA took over her life and lived it with her.

Stacey smiled to herself. At least her first date today could be without supervision. Tonight both she and Colin would feel the restraint of watching eyes, listening ears. Could they really get acquainted with a CIA agent between them?

She felt her heart tug between tall, blond, and tender Ken and the less-known, but exciting, tall, and dark Colin. Last night it seemed her heart was more taken by Ken. She'd been sorry about the date with Colin. Yet . . . yet she looked forward to tonight's date with a certain eagerness.

Scooping up her binoculars and bird book, she eased out of her room and tiptoed down the stairs. She filled her jacket pockets with bread and grabbed a couple of bananas. She scribbled a note to her mother, "Bird watching with Ken. Back by eight. I'll do the vacuuming today."

She sighed in relief as the front door closed behind her. She'd escaped without waking either her mom or Miriam.

She huddled on the front step to wait for Ken.

He pulled up at five-thirty on the dot. She ran out and slid onto the seat. "Away, quickly away," she chanted, laughing. "Hurry."

She watched the house over her shoulder as Ken pulled into the street. Nothing stirred. "We made it," she crowed, sliding down and getting comfortable.

"What's all this about?" Ken asked. "Didn't you tell your mother where you were going?" He slowed as though he were going to stop and take her back.

"I left them a note," she said. "It'll be all right."

"Then why the dramatics?"

"Starting today, the CIA is going to remain as close to me as my shadow." Stacey told him of the possible kidnapping attempt the night before. "They aren't taking any chances, so one of them will be with me all the time until they solve this case."

While she talked, Ken headed out of town. Now he slowed and pulled to the side of the road. "I'm not certain we should be going this morning, Stacey. It sounds as if you'd be safer at home."

"Oh, Ken. They just don't want me to be alone. I'm with you. No one is going to bother me. Besides, who'd be out and about at this time of the morning other than bird watchers?"

Ken hesitated, then swung back onto the road. "Okay. I hope I don't have some angry agents breathing down my neck threatening a life sentence for letting you talk me into this."

"They won't. Promise." Stacey pulled a banana from her pocket. "Half?"

He turned to look and smiled. "Sure. Though I've heard the odor of banana in the human system draws mosquitoes."

"It does?"

"I've never researched it myself, but someone told us that. Mom never buys bananas in the summertime. Mosquitoes love her anyway, and she doesn't want to encourage them."

They parked in the usual spot, loaded up and headed into the woods. The early sun darted tentative rays between the limbs of alders and vine maples. The only sounds were their own footfalls, the morning songs of a variety of birds, and a slight breeze rustling the tree tops.

I'm glad I came, thought Stacey. *It's a wonderful morning and just being with Ken is fun.* She looked up at him, and he smiled. Her heart tugged in response.

They walked along in companionable silence until they reached the offshoot path they'd followed the week before. "Same place?" asked Ken.

"We had pretty good luck there," Stacey replied. "But we might go a little farther in."

They found a promising site and set up. Ken took a few pictures of the general area, adjusting and readjusting his camera. They were sitting quietly when Stacey heard it.

Slowly, gently, she touched Ken's arm.

He looked at her inquiringly, and she mimed a listening attitude. He cocked his head to one side. "What?" he mouthed.

Stacey pointed to the book open on her lap, her finger tracing the description of the *Psaltriparus minimus* song. It grew louder, more insistent. She held her breath. Would they come out where she could see them?

Ken eased into a better position behind the camera and Stacey remained statue still except for her eyes, which searched the woods.

Eight to ten tiny brown birds with tails almost as long as their bodies flitted into a bush just a few feet to their left, gabbling among themselves. Several more arrived, but not before the first had darted to a vine maple branch.

Stacey wondered if their constant chatter contained news of the day, food finds, love notes, or what.

Suddenly their calls stopped. The birds rose in flight and winged deeper into the woods.

Stacey looked around and gasped. Arnold Tenley stood behind her. She jumped to her feet, book and binoculars sliding to the ground. She backed toward Ken, seeking protection.

"What are. . . ?" Her voice quavered. She stopped, gulped, started again, steadier this time. "What are you doing here?"

"Just came to take you for a ride."

"I don't want to ride with you. Thanks, but I'll pass." Her attempt at flippancy made his heavy lips curve in a humorless smile.

"Oh, you'll come, all right. There's no crowd around this morning."

Ken's hand gripped her shoulder. "Stacey said she didn't want to go with you. She's in my care this morning, and I'll see that she gets home."

"You think so?" A contemptuous glance raked Ken from foot to head. "I don't." He raised his voice. "Jake."

Stacey and Ken whirled. Another man stepped out from behind a fir. Ken looked from one to another, then took a couple of steps toward Jake, whose bearded face sat atop massive shoulders and a heavy body.

In that instant, Tenley grabbed Stacey from behind. She kicked out at him, striking his shin. He grunted and tightened his hold, lifting her off the ground, so she had no leverage to kick again. She twisted and struggled, but Tenley's grip only became firmer, holding her motionless against him.

Because he held her from behind, she couldn't hit or bite. She let herself go slack, hoping he'd let go like the villain always did in the stories, but Tenley jerked her upright.

Ken stood uncertainly between the two men, his glance shifting from one to the other. He turned his back on Tenley and headed for Jake, who strode forward to meet him.

"No, Ken. Run," Stacey called. "Run. Get help."

But Ken had already swung at Jake, his fist landing a

glancing blow as Jake shifted to one side.

Stacey flinched as Jake punched Ken in the stomach. As Ken doubled in pain, Jake hit him in the jaw. Ken fell to the ground.

Stacey thrashed helplessly as she struggled to get free. "Ken," she called. "Ken, are you all right?"

Tenley laughed and swung her around. "That'll keep him out of our business for a while. Meanwhile, we'll take that ride I mentioned."

"You're—you're not going to leave him there." Stacey twisted to see Tenley's face. "You can't. He might die . . . or, or . . ."

Tenley ignored her plea. He tried to march her down the path, but Stacey made herself go limp, refusing to stay upright or put one foot in front of the other. Maybe she could break away and get back to Ken. Besides, she wasn't about to make this easy for Tenley.

But Tenley didn't seem to care. "If you won't walk, you'll ride," he growled. "Jake."

Jake strode up, grabbed her, and tossed her over his shoulder as though she weighed nothing. It was extremely uncomfortable. Her hanging head bobbed with every step, her hip bone rubbed against Jake's shoulder.

She was about to offer to walk when a thought came. They couldn't take her out of the woods this way. One of the families on the dead-end road would be sure to report such a thing. So she endured the discomfort.

Then her eyes were caught by a worn leather case, smaller than a billfold that stuck out of Jake's pocket. Each step seemed to bring it higher. Yet she was afraid to reach out and drag it from his pocket. He might feel it.

Step by step she watched it. Sometimes it rose only to fall back again. Her heart in her mouth, she was reaching to pull the case when Jake stopped and heaved her higher on his shoulder. Automatically she grabbed at his back to steady herself, then recognizing her opportunity, slid the case from his pocket.

She held her breath for a moment, the case in her hand. She didn't dare open it. She'd just drop it and hope Ken or someone would pick it up and there'd be something in it to lead them to her.

She waited, hoping Jake and Tenley would exchange comments so she could drop the case under cover of their voices, but they stomped solidly through the woods. She decided she couldn't wait any longer, pretended a cough and let it go.

She almost screamed in exasperation. The case fell in a puddle of water. No one would ever find it there. Those puddles didn't dry out even in the hottest days of a Puget Sound summer.

When they came to the end of the trail, Jake swung her down and both men grabbed her by the arm. "Walk now," Tenley ordered. "Walk like we're good friends, out for morning exercise. If you try to break away or make any noise—a scream or yell—Jake'll go back and make sure your boyfriend never interferes again. Got it?"

Stacey nodded. She'd endure anything to keep Ken from being hurt anymore. Her heart squeezed. It was all her fault that he lay in the woods, maybe dead already. Jake had hit him awfully hard. Ken hadn't moved a muscle after he hit the ground.

Tears misted her eyes as she walked between the two men toward the gray panel truck parked behind Ken's old Volvo. Tenley held her while Jake unlocked the back doors, then they boosted her inside.

As soon as they closed the doors behind her, she crouched ready to spring, her hand poised over the handle. When they started around the truck to get in front, she'd jump and run for the nearest house. The instant she heard footsteps grating on the gravel, she jerked at the handle. Nothing happened.

She sank back in the corner of the truck, her thoughts churning madly. She took several deep breaths to ease the fear. Jake and Tenley were in the cab, Jake driving. She crawled forward.

"What do you think you'll accomplish by taking me?" Stacey sneered, feeling traitorous to her new relationship with her mother, but she had to try. "If you'd done any checking, you'd know that neither Mom or Dad would miss me all that much. They're not going to pay any great sums of money to get me back—even if they had it. They don't."

Jake turned and grinned at Tenley. The smile had nothing of humor in it. "That's an idea, boss. Should we demand a few thousand bucks to get her back?"

"Nah. What's a paltry fifty, sixty thousand? We'll have all the money we want when she talks and her folks come across with the information."

"What information?" Stacey demanded.

"Has to do with a project of your father's." Tenley paused before adding, "A project of your father's and the good ol' government."

"You're crazy," Stacey accused. "Dad would never tell you anything about a project he's working on. I tell you any one of his projects is far more important to him that I am, ever was, or ever will be."

"Yeah?"

"Yeah." Stacey leaned forward. "So, if you'll let me go, I won't say a word about this. I won't report it or anything. You gain nothing by taking me, except maybe a prison term for kidnapping. You lose nothing by letting me go."

"Forget it, kid. Your parents will come across."

Stacey tried to find a comfortable spot on the corrugated metal floor. *If only I'd stayed home*, she thought. *If only I hadn't wanted my one last fling at freedom—time alone with Ken. He wouldn't be lying back there hurt.* She wouldn't let herself think it could be any worse. *Mom wouldn't be in for hours of worry and agents Riley, Dicks, and Miriam wouldn't be furious with me.*

I blew it, she harangued herself. *If only I'd been obedient.* The word touched off a new chain of thought. God— God was here with her, even though she'd done the wrong thing in sneaking out this morning.

Stacey leaned her head against the side of the truck and closed her eyes. "God," she whispered. "It's all my own fault that I'm in this mess. What I did was wrong. Will you please get me out? Don't let Mom be frantic. Don't let Dad have to give away government secrets. Show me what to do."

Somehow comforted, Stacey leaned forward, her arms crossed on her drawn-up knees, her head resting on her arms.

She sat quietly when the van finally came to a stop. After a muttering of voices at Jake's window, she heard a scraping noise, then a squeal. A gate being opened? They drove only a short distance, then stopped.

Jake stayed at the wheel while Tenley came around and unlocked the back doors. Stacey felt there was no point in resisting now. She got to her feet and jumped to the ground. Tenley grabbed her arm.

They were in a farmyard. A weatherbeaten post and pole fence staggered around a field more filled with rusty farm equipment than grass or hay. The barn roof sagged despondently over grayed walls spotted with frequent gaps where boards had fallen helter-skelter amidst more rusty tools.

The two-story farm house appeared in better condition. Ancient green paint was chipped and peeling, but the walls stood straight and solid. The dirty, glass-filled windows neither invited nor welcomed.

Arnold Tenley marched her toward the door while Jake parked the van in a tumbledown shed close to the barn.

Stacey had no opportunity to see much of the house. As soon as they entered the back door onto a sort of porch, Tenley pushed her to the right and up a steep, narrow staircase. Three doors opened off the square hall at the top.

Tenley reached around her and flung open the one on the right. He propelled her inside and growled, "It's home, kid, until your dad comes through. May as well get comfortable."

Stacey stood by the door, closed and locked from the

other side by Tenley. The room was small. A single bed with a rough brown blanket, a small, scarred wooden dresser, and a kitchen chair almost filled it. A pair of grimy windows let in a little of the morning light.

Choking back a sob of fear, Stacey tiptoed toward the window. Boards creaked beneath her feet, broadcasting, she was sure, every movement to whoever else was in the house. Jake would probably be downstairs by now. She wondered who else might be there—Neva? Charlie? Were there others?

She leaned against the window molding and looked out. It was one of the windows she'd seen from the drive. The same dismal view offered no hope or cheer.

"Oh, God," she prayed. "What do I do now? Why was I so stupid as to insist on going out this morning? Help me."

She tried to raise the window, but it wouldn't budge. She was about to give up, but saw the simple swing lock that held the window. She forced it back and tried again. This time the window slid up. She leaned out and breathed in fresh air, a contrast to the stuffy, closed-in smell of the room.

Hope of escape welled, but only for a moment. Leaning out and looking down, she saw a long drop to a concrete parking pad. If she tried to jump, she'd probably break an ankle and be in even worse trouble.

Leaving the window open to the welcome breeze and the sounds of cars going by on a distant road, Stacey approached the bed. She picked up a corner of the blanket between thumb and forefinger and pulled it back. The printed sheets looked crisp and new—the only pleasant thing since Tenley scared off the birds. Maybe she'd crawl in and make up for the lost sleep this morning.

But fear and remorse were too great to allow sleep. *Ken*, she thought, *what have I done to you? Are you all right?* Even thoughts of Ken faded as she began to feel ravenous. Would they feed her?

Almost as if her thoughts had conjured up reality, she heard a key turn in the shiny new brass lock. She slid out from the covers and sat cross-legged on top. Then she bounded to the floor. If the person was bringing food, he'd have his hands full, and maybe she could push him down and get by, down the stairs and out the door.

The door swung inward. *Charlie*—Charlie with a black-and-blue eye and puffy lips—held a tray as Tenley stood behind him, key in hand. Tenley waited until Charlie was in, then closed and relocked the door.

Charlie set the tray on the dresser. Stacey noticed his wrists were red and raw.

"Charlie! What happened?"

He glared at her. "*You*—that's what happened! This is the result of being taken in by a kid, falling for the glow in a pair of innocent looking blue eyes."

Stacey reached up and gently touched the bruised cheek-bone.

He flinched.

"I'm sorry, Charlie. Was it because you tried to sneak me out of that restaurant?"

"Yeah. Instead of being one of the kingpins, in line for my share of millions, I'm a prisoner—because of you. They'll kill me when I'm no use to them anymore."

"They wouldn't really kill anyone, would they?" Fear trembled in Stacey's voice.

"Most people would kill for several million dollars. This crowd isn't any exception." Charlie ran his hand through his brown hair and down his neck. "Why didn't I just go through with it? I'd have been smarter to let you be taken and try to save you here."

"It wouldn't have worked. Two CIA agents were there watching. Even if you'd gone through with the plan, it would have been stopped."

He stared at her, anger flaring in his brown eyes. "You mean I lost a chance at over a million bucks for nothing?"

For a moment, Stacey thought he would hit her. Suddenly the anger died, and Charlie started to laugh. Stacey stared helplessly while Charlie's eyes streamed with tears and he doubled over, clutching his sides.

When he could talk again, he gasped, "Serves me right. Step out of character and it'll do you in every time." He gestured to the tray. "It's not much, but you'd better eat something."

The tray held a plate of toast, a jar of peanut butter, a table knife, and two cups of coffee. Stacey sat cross-legged on the bed again. Charlie set the tray down beside her, took one cup, and sat on the chair. He lifted the cup. "Cheers."

Stacey smeared peanut butter on the cold toast and munched half a piece before she asked, "What are the chances of getting out of here?"

"None." He turned over his wrists. "I found out. Every door is locked with a dead bolt and all the windows on the first floor are nailed shut. The filth on the outside hides heavy mesh screens on the inside."

"What happened to your wrists?"

"I'd almost pried off the screen in a pantry when Neva found me. Since then, I've been tied in the room next to this one."

"Why are you out now?"

"I convinced them I wouldn't try to escape if I could get a chance to get even with you." He looked at her with a strange expression in his eyes. "And now I can't do it. I'm not even mad any more. What is it about you, Stacey?"

Stacey took a swallow of tepid coffee before she answered. "I guess the same answer I gave last night . . . Jesus."

Noises outside the room drew their attention. Tenley shoved the door open, and he and Neva Boyce stepped into the crowded room. Tenley closed the door and leaned against it as Neva advanced a couple of steps.

"Okay, let's have it. The truth now."

Stacey stared at her. "The truth about what?"

"Where your father is." Neva's cold amber eyes bored into Stacey, as if she could see inside her brain to drag out the information she demanded.

"But we've told you over and over. Dad's in Denver. He's working at the government lab there. We gave—"

"You gave us nothing. A name, a phone number for a lab in Seattle, another lab in Denver. You don't really expect us to believe that story."

Stacey broke the hypnotic stare of the older woman and looked from Tenley to Charlie. Both looked at her as if she would come up with some fabulous answer that would help them hit the jackpot. She shook her head.

"I don't know what you're talking about. Dad's a physicist. You know that. He works for the lab in Seattle. He works for the government in Denver on occasion. That's what he's doing now. Why can't you accept that?"

Charlie's eyes pleaded with her. "Stacey, we know. You can tell the truth."

She stared back at him. "I don't understand. What's so unbelievable about Dad's being in Denver?"

"Cut the lies." Neva moved to stand over Stacey like a vulture ready to attack. "We know your Dad is CIA."

"Dad? CIA? You're crazy!" Stacey laughed in spite of the fingers of fear that raced up and down her spine. "CIA is the last thing my staid old dad would be."

Stacey flinched as Neva brought her hand up and started to swing. Charlie reached out and grabbed Neva's wrist. "That's not going to accomplish anything, Ms. Boyce. Can't you see she's telling the truth? She doesn't know."

Chapter Fourteen

Neva turned her fury on Charlie. "Let go of me. Who do you think you are—traitor?" She reached out to rake his face with the nails of her other hand, but Charlie grabbed that wrist, too, and held her easily.

She twisted helplessly for a moment, then lifted her chin and demanded, her voice icy and cutting, "Arnold, why are you just standing there?"

Stacey looked at Tenley and surprised a smirk on his squashed-in face. It disappeared immediately, and he swaggered over. He reached out a hand and grabbed the front of Charlie's shirt. "Let the lady go. Or would you like a second purple eye?"

Charlie dropped Neva's wrists. Tenley tightened his grasp and pulled Charlie toward him. "Hands off, scum. I've a mind to—"

"Enough, Arnold. We'll take care of him later." Neva massaged her wrists. "Right now, I want the truth out of this kid."

Arnold let go and moved back against the door. "I can shake her up a bit. But I think soft-headed Charlie's right. She doesn't know."

"The idea of my dad's being CIA is ridiculous. He's as straight as an arrow. No tricks, no subterfuge—ever. He just doesn't fit."

150

"He's been with the CIA for years." Neva moved over to the door. "You have to know if you've a brain in your head. In some ways, you're pretty sharp. That makes you a liar."

Stacey's voice was as cold and hard as Neva's. "If *you* had any smarts," she sneered, "you could recognize truth when you hear it."

Stacey stood up while she taunted Neva. Now she backed toward the window at the hatred in Neva's amber eyes. They stared at one another for a long moment, then Neva took a step forward.

The tension was broken as Tenley jingled the keys. "Let's let her think about it for a while," he advised. "If she knows anything, she'll come across before too many hours go by."

Neva stared at Stacey until Tenley swung open the door and touched her shoulder. She turned and stalked toward the hall. "Yes. We have a ransom note to write."

Charlie and Stacey watched the door close behind the two and heard the lock click into place.

"That wasn't very wise, Stacey." Charlie lowered himself into the chair. "You're in enough trouble without making a personal enemy of Neva. She's vindictive."

Stacey curled up on the end of the bed. "It wasn't very nice either. I sounded like I used to before Jesus forgave me. I wish I hadn't said it."

"She provoked you, but don't let it get to you again."

"Do they really believe Dad's a CIA agent?"

"Not an agent, an occasional courier. He carries documents and delivers them."

"I can't believe that of my dad. He's so . . . so conservative."

"He's also loyal and patriotic. Some people—like your father—believe so strongly in things important to them, they do things they'd rather not do."

"Like what you're doing?"

"No. I was in this for money, only money." He shrugged

his shoulders. "A lot of good it's going to do me now."

Stacey went to look out the window. She turned and faced Charlie. "You're sure Dad's a courier?"

"Yes."

"Then he's in danger?"

"Those who take these jobs know the possibilities."

"If Neva and Tenley find him, they'll kill him?"

"Only if he won't turn over what he's carrying."

"What's that?" Stacey held her breath. Would he tell her?

Charlie stared at her for a long minute. "We're almost certain an agent got a message through to someone before that agent died. We're not sure to whom. We've got to stop that message from getting any farther."

"But it's been two weeks. Surely it's been passed on to everyone concerned by now."

"We don't think so. I admit it's puzzled us. Maybe the code hasn't been deciphered. Maybe the interim link bungled somehow. Maybe . . . maybe a lot of things. But if the message had gotten through, we'd know it. There would be frantic activity in some of the world capitals."

"What is the message?"

He hesitated a moment more. "You'll be here until it's all over, so no reason not to tell you." A touch of braggadocio crept into his voice. "You've heard of the African Council meeting called for early July in Geneva? Because of what we know about the agent who died, we're fairly certain one of three couriers will be used to pass his information."

"My dad is one of them?"

"Yes." Charlie went on, "We can't let that evidence get through. It would wipe out months of planning, months of practice, months of conditioning a team to assassinate Teldake, the emerging leader from one of those small African countries. He's powerful, a favorite of his people, and very pro-American. Lots of leaders in that part of the world don't want to see him in power."

Stacey had been staring out the window as he talked. Now she whirled to face him. "And you're helping to stop the word that would save his life?"

"If he lives, he'll upset the balance of power. Our people don't want that."

"Then defeat him in elections, through—" Stacey stopped, staring at Charlie. "Our people? You mean you don't believe in democracy, in the rights we have in America? You live here and enjoy all the benefits, but support our enemies? You're a traitor?"

The word—thrown at Charlie for the second time within minutes—quivered on the air between them.

He studied his fingernails for what seemed several minutes before he finally looked up and answered Stacey. "It's not that so much. It's who makes it worthwhile. These people pay and pay well. My cut—if I still get a cut—would be more than six hundred grand. I need the money."

"And you're still loyal, even though you think they're planning to kill you?"

"That's my fault. I was tricked by your innocent story. I'm getting what I deserve."

"But if you helped me escape, if you gave your evidence to the CIA, you could prevent all this. Surely the government would take care of you."

"That's all you know. With my record, I'd be in worse trouble in their hands. Here, if I continue to cooperate, I may still get my cut. With the CIA, I'd rot in prison."

Stacey looked out at the sunshine gilding the jumble of rusty equipment. She ached to jump and run—to protect her father. Her thoughts raced. *Was Charlie right? Did Dad carry papers for the CIA? Or were they mistaking him for someone else?* She turned to look at Charlie. He was deadly serious. He, at least, was convinced her dad was a courier.

Both Charlie and Stacey looked at the door as the key turned in the lock. Jake stood in the opening. "Okay, Charlie. Time for your incomparable talents. Let's go."

Charlie smiled wryly. "See? I'm needed. I'm still in the

game." He pulled something from his breast pocket and tossed it to Stacey. "You probably could use this."

Stacey caught her blue New Testament and clasped it tightly. "Thanks."

She heard Jake say, "Any funny business and—" Jake pulled the door closed, cutting off the rest of the threat.

For a long time Stacey stood by the window, staring sightlessly at the concrete below. Was it all true? She couldn't believe it; yet Charlie was so sure, so serious, so certain he told the truth.

Stacey shivered. If it were true, she had to get out of here. She had to warn her dad, to get agents Riley and Dicks doing something to stop both her dad's part in the plot and the assassination.

If she could somehow contact them, there'd be no need for her dad to carry a sealed, coded message to agents hiding in dark alleys.

She leaned out the window, gauging the concrete surface below. If only she had a rope. She turned and yanked the blanket off the bed. She'd tear the sheets into strips, tie them together and lower herself down.

But the crisp, new sheet failed to rip. Her hands weren't strong enough to even stretch it. She pulled out the dresser drawers, searching for something to cut with, but each was empty. She even tried chewing a hole, but the closely woven fabric resisted her efforts.

Defeated, she sank in the middle of the bed. Tears of frustration welled in her eyes and she dashed them away with her fist. She wouldn't give up. Somehow she'd get out of here.

She paced over to the door and tried it. She had hoped they had forgotten to lock it, but no such luck. Walking back to the window, she leaned out and yelled at the top of her lungs. "Help. I've been kidnapped. Help. Call the police."

Heavy footsteps slammed up the steps and the key rattled in the lock. The door flung open and Jake crossed the room in three strides. His beefy hand slashed out and struck her across the face, sending her reeling against the bed.

Stacey stared at him defiantly while her left hand crept up to soothe her bruised cheek.

"Try that again, brat, and you'll be tied and gagged." Jake stared at her. His small eyes, squished into his broad, bearded face, threatened.

Stacey trembled and remained silent.

Jake broke his stare and glanced around the room. He sneered as he grabbed up the sheets. "Doesn't seem you're to be trusted." With no apparent effort, he ripped one down the middle. "Can't have you swinging out the window with these." He bundled them under his arm. "These would work to hog-tie someone who can't be trusted." His hands worked as though he were already tying the knots.

"No, please," Stacey whispered. "I won't yell again." *Please God*, she prayed silently. *Don't let him. I'd never have a chance to escape.* Aloud she added, "I promise— on this." She held up her New Testament.

"Oh, yeah? Anyway, see you keep your word. I only warn once."

Stacey was actually glad to see the door close and hear the lock click. Jake frightened her—much more than the others. She rubbed her cheek.

For a while she stood staring out the window, not really seeing, her mind running in circles trying to think of a way out. After a long time, she threw the blanket over the bare mattress and sat down.

Ken. Was he all right? Was he still lying in the woods or had he regained consciousness? Would he go to her home? Would he give the alarm? What would he do in her predicament? The answer that came brought comfort. He'd talk to God about it—maybe read the Bible.

She picked up her New Testament and leafed idly through the pages, seeking a word of hope, something to wipe out the despair caused by Jake and his threats.

As she got into the Psalms at the back of the book, she remembered the verse her mother had read to her. Maybe she could find it. It was something about God being a help in trouble.

Starting at the beginning Psalm, she skimmed through each chapter. She paused and reread the first verse of Psalm 27: "The Lord is my light and my salvation—whom shall I fear? The Lord is the stronghold of my life—of whom shall I be afraid?"

It wasn't the one her mother had read, but it eased the tension. More slowly now, with less desperation, she skimmed on while in the back of her mind the phrase "whom shall I fear?" repeated itself. Did it really mean she didn't have to fear anyone? Even Jake or Neva?

Then she found it, the forty-sixth Psalm. "God is our refuge and strength, an ever present help in trouble." She went on reading that she needn't fear even if the earth gave way or the mountains quaked or fell into the sea. The turmoil inside her *felt* that cataclysmic.

She relaxed in the comfort of the words. Tucking the Testament under her bruised cheek, she curled up and dropped off to sleep.

The unlocking of her door woke her. She jerked upright, looking around her in perplexity. Then the memories rushed back. A glance at her watch confirmed the shadows outside. Six o'clock. She'd slept all afternoon.

The sight of the tray in the hands of a woman she hadn't seen before made her realize she was famished. She'd only had half a banana and a piece of toast since early morning.

The short, gray-haired woman shoved the tray onto the dresser. "Come on. I'll take you to the bathroom." She paused at the doorway. "Please. Don't try to escape. My life is hard enough. Don't make it worse."

Something pathetic about the weary face dried up the ideas dancing in Stacey's imagination. She was sure she could overpower the little woman and perhaps get away. But the pleading eyes and hopeless voice wouldn't let her do it.

With a tender sensitivity new to her, Stacey reached out and touched the woman's shoulder. "I won't. Is it possible to get a comb and a toothbrush?"

"I've already set them out. Feel free to use anything you need." She sighed tiredly. "They've removed everything you might use to get away or even hurt them with, so just take care of your needs. I'll be waiting right here."

Stacey entered the bathroom. A shower stall, toilet, and sink were crowded into a tiny windowless room that probably had once been a closet.

She felt somewhat better when she stepped out, her mouth fresh and her hair in place. The woman followed her back to the room and was about to close the door and leave when Stacey asked, "Aren't you going to stay?"

"No. They'll think I've been gone too long already.They're waiting for me to serve their dinner. Jake will be mad if I don't hurry."

"And you're afraid of Jake—like I am?"

Pain crossed the woman's face as she nodded. "My own son—and I think he'd kill me if I didn't do what he says. Yes, I'm afraid." Her body seemed to shrink. "I don't know what happened. He used to be such a good boy."

Stacey had a hard time picturing Jake as a young boy, much less a good kid. Even with the disguise of the beard, his face was hard and cruel. She rubbed her cheek, remembering his violent reaction to her yelling.

"I'm sorry," she whispered, again touching the woman's shoulder. "You'd better lock my door and go."

Stacey took the tray over to the bed. Homemade beef vegetable soup steamed in an insulated bowl. Crisp celery and carrots shared a plate with a stack of soda crackers. A glass of milk completed the meal, but the final touch was a single wild rose nestled on the white cloth covering the bottom of the tray. This simple, but eloquent, attempt at decency touched Stacey deeply.

Despite her anxiety, she ate with relish, enjoying every bite. Jake's mother was a good cook. But more, she was a compassionate lady. Stacey lifted the rose and drew in its fragrance. It was comforting to know she had a friend in the house, even though the friend could do nothing for her.

No, that wasn't true. Jake's mother had given her a delicious meal, tastefully served. Her spirits were lighter because of the thoughtfulness. She even dared to hope that something might happen to get her out before it was too late—too late for her dad and for the new African leader.

What was her mother doing now? She'd be frantic. Had they notified her dad? Would he fly home? Surely Ken was safe by now. Was Miriam with her mother or out looking for Stacey? Would they go to the woods to search? Would they find that folder of Jake's? Would it lead them to her?

These questions and more raced round and round through her head. Some she thought she knew the answers to, others she could only guess. Exhausted from trying to work it out, she fell asleep again.

In her dreams, she heard the roar of a large truck and raging voices. Gradually coming awake, she realized it wasn't a dream. Several men were arguing outside her window. They weren't shouting. She couldn't even distinguish the words, but fury permeated their rough voices.

She crept from the bed to the window and knelt to listen.

"Fool!" one voice, icy in its anger, condemned. "A simple task. Just pick up White and get him out."

"If it were so simple," a hot angry voice replied, "why didn't you do it?"

"That's what you're paid for," chimed in a third voice.

"Hey. Listen to the facts." It was Charlie's voice. "We couldn't get near him. There were so many agents around, you'd think he was the president of the United States. No one could have taken him."

"You could have shot him." Stacey thought it was Tenley who said that.

"Then we'd have all this work to do over with another courier," snapped Neva. "My orders were no killing. Not at this point."

Relief swept over Stacey. They hadn't been able to reach her dad. Peering beyond the frame, she risked a glance out the window. Pre-dawn light barely revealed the grimy fields and the people below. Jake, Charlie, Neva, Tenley, and two men she didn't recognize were moving away from a big van, much larger than the one she'd arrived in, backed below her window.

She jerked her hand to her mouth to stifle the gasp that involuntarily jerked from her lungs when she realized how close the truck was. She could step out the window, drop no more than three feet onto the top of the truck, climb down over the hood and be gone.

She held her breath, watching the conspirators to make sure none had heard and spotted her watching from the window. Apparently they hadn't. Light spilled out the door and six shadows crossed inside before the closing door snuffed out the light.

Stacey waited for a few heart-stopping moments to make sure they remained inside, then cautiously pushed up the window frame. She eased her right leg over the sill, ducking her head and shoulders under the top frame.

The truck was too far away. She couldn't make the step. She might miss and go hurtling on down to the cement. A noise below made her freeze—half in, half out the window.

It was only a cat. She wiggled back inside the house, put both legs out the window, then twisted over on her stomach. Her searching feet felt the top of the van.

Carefully, silently, she let herself down. She shoved off with her hands, teetered for a moment, then caught her balance.

The top of the truck gave with each step, creaking slightly. It only took a moment to reach the front. She sat on the edge, stood on the top of the cab, then down to the hood, to the bumper and to the ground.

Casting a quick glance around, excitement pounding in her chest, Stacey turned left and started for the road.

"Going somewhere?" Tenley stepped in front of her. The first rays of sunlight caught and reflected off the barrel of an enormous hand gun aimed at her.

Her heart stood still, then plummeted to her feet. She sagged dejectedly. He must have heard the gasp.

He waved the gun at her. "Back in the house."

She stepped around the cab of the truck several paces in front of him. A surge of hope lent wings to her feet, she dashed the length of the truck. When she rounded the corner of the house, hoping for cover, she found Charlie. She ran right into him, knocking the breath from her lungs. He grabbed her in his arms. She moved with him assuming he was again aiding her escape. Instead, he walked her to the back door of the house and shoved her inside.

Jake stood at the foot of the narrow stairs, strips of her printed sheets hanging over his shoulder. Stacey thought she read satisfaction, even delight in his small, close-set eyes.

Unresisting, she climbed the stairs and waited at the door until he unlocked it. She heard the truck roar as someone drove it away from her window.

She turned to face Jake. "You don't have to tie me. There's no way I can get out the window now."

"We'll make sure of that." Roughly and painfully he bound her arms behind her back. Another strip of colorful sheet tied her ankles together. He tossed her on the bed. "That should keep you."

Tears coursed down her cheeks. Not only had she failed, she'd reduced what freedom she'd had. She couldn't even read her New Testament or see her watch. The desire to know the time grew as she lay alone through a long morning and into the afternoon.

As the moments dragged by, clouds covered the skies. She tried to evade her gloomy thoughts by thinking of what she'd be doing if these people hadn't invaded her life.

She would have been at church with Becky. She'd miss the sermon. Maybe she could get a tape of it later. She hated the thought of losing one bit of information. Today one of the agents would have been sitting in the pew with her or maybe behind her.

She wondered what Colin had thought when he stopped

to pick her up last night. Would anyone have told him she was missing or did they say she was sick? She even smiled a little when she wondered how he would have felt about having an agent accompany them.

Ken . . . Ken would have joked and laughed about it. She remembered his warm hand holding hers when they were first introduced, the twinkle in his gray-green eyes as he bent to look at her. More pictures flashed in her memory: Ken teaching, Ken guiding her gently with a hand at her back, Ken's face as he watched the mountain beaver parade across the clearing, Ken as he soothed her mother's fears.

Pain washed over her at thoughts of her mother. How would she endure this? She hoped her dad had come home. Would he agree to lead the spies to the agents? He just couldn't give the spies the message meant to abort the assassination. She prayed he wouldn't put her safety before the life of a possible new world leader.

She turned restlessly, winced at the pain, and twisted to find a more comfortable way to lie. "Oh, God, help. I know you can work miracles. Please get me out of here. Free me before Dad has to make such an awful decision."

Stacey struggled to a sitting position, which helped ease the strain in her shoulders. Her hands were numb, her feet and legs asleep. Besides, she was hungry. That she might be able to do something about. Sliding off the bed Stacey began hopping up and down, to the door and back, to the window, the door again, then to the bed.

Panting with her effort, she sank on the edge of the bed. She was rewarded with the sound of footsteps mounting the stairs. Slow, tired footsteps.

Jake's mother called through the door. "What's wrong?"

Stacey hopped over to the door. "I'm hungry. Aren't you going to feed me?"

"Not until Jake gets back."

"Please. I won't try to escape."

"Jake and Neva have the keys. You'll have to wait."

Her voice faded as though she were turning away. Then Stacey heard her descending the stairs.

She hopped to the window. A light drizzle fell like slow tears from gray skies. The neglected farm equipment looked even more desolate. Stacey leaned her forehead against the window and wept with the rain.

Chapter Fifteen

Her tears couldn't last as long as the rain. When they had spent themselves, she hopped back to the bed. Not to sleep, but to fruitlessly plan ways of escape.

After a long time, she heard someone climbing the stairs. The footsteps sounded different—not the heavy tread of Jake, nor the slow, tired steps of his mother. These were light and quick.

A glimmer of hope flickered in Stacey. Maybe someone was coming to rescue her. When the door open and Neva stepped inside, that hope died.

Neva walked over and knelt beside the bed, a look of concern on her normally cold face. Gently she untied the sheets binding Stacey. She even massaged her wrists to help return circulation.

Stacey didn't understand her sudden change to kindness. "Thanks," she said, not quite trusting this new attitude. "Why?"

"Jake overdoes everything. Always wants the most violent means of accomplishing our purposes." She picked up the strips of fabric, dropped them in the waste basket. "Those aren't necessary."

She turned back to Stacey, a smile warming her face. "Why don't I stay with you long enough for you to have a warm, relaxing shower?"

Stacey could only stare. She wasn't quite convinced. Why was Neva being so nice to her? She'd been in a terrific rage when she'd left the day before. But, the opportunity for a shower was too good to pass up.

"Thanks," she said again. "That would be great."

Neva walked with her to the bathroom, careful to stay between Stacey and the stairwell. "I have to lock you in— it's all my life is worth if I let you escape. When you're ready, just knock. I'll be here to let you out."

Stacey stepped into the cramped room, looking forward to a refreshing shower. A knock on the door was followed by Neva offering her some clean clothes. "You'll want these. They're mine, but they should fit well enough."

Stacey stood under the pelting water for a long time. The hot spray soothed the ache in her shoulders, helped her relax. She toweled herself dry, dressed and brushed her teeth. When her hair was dry and combed, she knocked on the door.

Neva opened it immediately. "You look better." Again staying between Stacey and the stairwell, Neva walked her back to the room, chatting about shampoos and cleansers, like any girlfriend might do.

She didn't seem in any hurry to leave. While Stacey curled on the end of the bed, Neva stretched out on the single chair in the room. Her fingers played with the tails of the silk tie on her stark white blouse.

"Tell me," Neva said, "about your plans. Do you really want to become a physicist?"

"Yes. I think it's one of the most exciting fields going. It has so much scope, so many possibilities." Stacey went on to describe some of the areas of particular interest to her.

Neva asked leading questions, keeping the conversation going for several minutes. She shared some of her goals and plans when she was just out of high school and which ones had and had not been fulfilled.

The talk drifted into boys and dates, fashions and brands of makeup—the things any two girls might discuss as they became acquainted.

At first Stacey was wary, waiting for a trap, a trick question. But after a while, she relaxed and almost forgot she was a prisoner with a desperate need to escape.

Her wariness returned when Neva asked, "Tell me about your family."

"We're sort of average," Stacey replied cautiously. "Dad's a scientist with a good job. Mom's a nurse and she works because she enjoys it—even the odd shifts." She hesitated a moment and decided not to mention her brothers and sister. If the gang didn't know about them, she wasn't going to put them in jeopardy by mentioning they existed. "Until you came into our lives a couple of weeks ago, we were a typical family—some misunderstandings, some problems, but with lots of good times, too."

"You didn't mention your brothers and sister," Neva prodded. "Aren't they all quite a bit older than you?"

So they knew. "Yes. I don't know them well. I was only four when Geoff left for school. Of course he came home for holidays and summers, but he didn't have much time for a baby sister." She sighed, remembering how excited she'd been to have all her older brothers and sister home. "I guess I know Wade best. I was quite a bit older before he took off."

"You must be proud of them all." Neva straightened, crossing one knee over the other.

"I never thought much about it," Stacey said. "They've never been a big part of my life."

"Do they know your father is a CIA courier?"

Here it is, thought Stacey. *The point of this two hour conversation. She's patient, you've got to give her that.* "I'm sure they don't. I don't know that he is. In fact, I strongly doubt it."

"But we know. We've told you."

"You've offered no proof. Only accu—" She broke off the harsh word, substituted, "statements."

"Would we risk keeping you here if we weren't one hundred per cent sure?"

Stacey shrugged. "Probably not, but that doesn't mean he is. You could be mistaken. I feel I've been especially close to Dad. It just doesn't fit his character."

Yet it did when she remembered what Charlie said. Dad would do something like that if he felt it was his duty, that it could best be accomplished by him.

Had Neva noticed a change in expression when the thought occurred to her? She stood and looked out the window. Rain still drizzled over the unkempt field and sagging outbuildings.

Trying to cover the growing certainty that her father might act as courier on occasion, Stacey added, "In fact, if you met him, you'd probably classify him as dull—except when it comes to science." *Forgive me, Dad*, she said silently. *I think you're grand.*

"You truly think your dad is in Colorado? That he's working on a physics project and nothing more?"

"That's right. We've been talking to him almost every day. I'm sure you're aware of that, too."

Neva's gaze riveted on Stacey. "Meaning?"

Stacey stared back, hoping she hadn't given away the fact that the family was aware of the bugs and phone tap. "Meaning you've been keeping pretty close tabs on us. I'm sure you know what's going on."

Neva discernibly relaxed. "It's our job. There's just one thing wrong with your argument."

"What?"

A small smile played across Neva's face. "When your dad calls, there's no way of telling where he's calling from. He could just as well be in New York, Mexico, or Paris."

"Surely you'd know if he left Colorado. I can't believe you don't keep as close track of him as you did of me."

"We haven't been following you."

"Then how did you know I'd be in the woods yesterday morning?" Concern for Ken flashed through her mind. Had he set her up, all the while pretending to be protective? No. Not someone who could teach about God the way he did.

Not someone whose eyes warmed you with a glance. Ken was okay.

"We lucked out. After that guy who claimed to be your brother butted in Friday night, Tenley thought it might be good to keep an eye on you." Neva's old cold smile replaced the fake warmth she'd been exuding. "We almost missed you, didn't dream you'd make such an early start."

Neva stood and stretched. "It's been interesting, but not particularly informative. Maybe you don't know anything, but I wouldn't stake my life on it." She walked to the door, then paused. "Don't try anything stupid. I've left you untied. I won't do that again if you try another escape."

Stacey stared at the closing door. Had she given anything away? Had there been trick questions she hadn't noticed? What had Neva learned?

"God, help me not to say anything to harm anyone," she prayed. "And please, show me a way to get out, to warn Dad and agent Riley."

She paced to the window, then turned back into the room. The scene outside was too depressing. It only made her feel worse.

Within minutes, she heard Jake's mother's steps on the stairs. At last she would get some food. It seemed ages since the bowl of hot soup last night.

Eagerly she awaited the opening of the door. She took the tray from the old woman and set it on the end of the bed. The aroma was delectable.

The woman lifted a warmer lid from a dinner plate to reveal a generous slice of pot roast, potatoes and gravy, broccoli with cheese sauce and a pickled beet. Another small plate held a crisp salad. Again the white cloth was decorated with a single wild rose.

"Thank you," she said. "This looks delicious. You're a good cook."

"Ought to be. Ran a restaurant for years," she snorted. "Thought I'd retired until Jake showed up again with this houseful of people." She sighed and shuffled wearily out the door. "Enjoy the dinner, deary."

"I will," Stacey told the closing door, her fork poised over the fluffy potatoes.

After she'd eaten, Stacey read her New Testament, reveling in the ability to use her hands again. Then she tried praying. She remembered everyone she could think of—her mother and father, the agents who would be trying to find her, Ken, even that leader who was to be assassinated sometime this week or next. She prayed urgently that God would save him somehow, even if she couldn't get free.

She slept fitfully that night. She'd taken off her jeans and sweatshirt, but the roughness of the bare mattress and the blanket made her itch. She endured it for a while, but at midnight she pulled on her clothes. They were less than comfortable, but better than the scratchy bed.

Waking early to the sound of pounding rain, she flopped over and pulled the blanket more closely around her, but sleep was gone. Stacey sat up and reached for her New Testament. Looking for reassurance, she decided to try to find the verses Ken and Becky had given her Thursday night about being a child of God, part of His family.

For a while she couldn't recall where in the Bible they'd directed her, and she flipped idly through the pages. Then she remembered that one was close to the place in Romans where she'd found the information on slaves.

Eagerly she turned back to chapter six and started reading. Just when she got to chapter eight and the verses she was looking for, the door opened and Jake's mother entered with a tray.

Stacey threw back the blanket and went to take it from her.

"It's not much this morning, just some oatmeal and toast," the woman apologized. "Jake wouldn't let me take time for anything more."

"This is great," Stacey soothed. "I thought I wouldn't get anything until tonight."

Hardly waiting for the closing door, Stacey scooped

brown sugar from a tiny yellow bowl onto the cereal and topped it with warmed milk from a matching pitcher.

After finishing breakfast, she read for a while, but eventually lost her concentration. When she couldn't sit still any longer, she stared through the window at the drizzle, all that was left of the early morning cloudburst.

Disheartened by the outside view, she tried pacing. The room was only seven steps long and five wide. *Not much exercise to that,* she thought. *I'll do some of the calisthenics we used to warm up for sports.*

After some stretching exercises, she went on to deep knee bends, sit ups, push ups, and jumping jacks. She'd only done a few when she heard a pounding, followed by an angry voice.

"Stop that jumping around. If you don't cut the noise, I'll hog-tie you to the bed."

Stacey grinned. She considered continuing, just to irritate, but discarded the thought. She didn't want to be tied again.

With nothing else to do, she lay down on the bed. Monday morning and no one had found her. Were they looking? Did they have any clues at all? Her one hope had been that someone would pick up Jake's leather case, that it contained something that would bring them to this place, but either they hadn't found it or there was no lead.

The thoughts depressed her as much as the gray drizzle outside. "Why, God?" she asked. "Why is this happening to us?"

Stacey passed the morning by alternately lying on the bed and doing quiet exercises. She read a great deal from her New Testament and prayed. Often her thoughts turned to Ken. How she wished she could see his comforting eyes, feel his warm hand on hers. Would she ever see him again?

Shortly after noon, Neva brought up a lunch tray with a beef sandwich, fresh vegetables, and a glass of milk. "By the way," she said as she stepped out the door, "your family has received our ransom note."

"I told you they don't have any money."

"And we told you we're not asking for money. Just information. When your dad turns over the sealed message he's supposed to deliver, we'll set you free." Neva paused, smiling her cold, cruel smile. "So if you're holding back anything, now's the time to spill it. It would save your dad an agonizing decision."

Stacey set the sandwich down on the tray. "I can't tell you what I don't know."

"Have it your way." Neva slammed the door behind her, grating the key in the lock as if to emphasize Stacey's prisoner status.

For a moment, Stacey stared at the door. Her impulse was to pound on it, yelling and screaming to get out. But she knew that would only result in being tied up again. If she were to get a chance to escape at all, she must maintain what freedom she had.

Ignoring lunch, she paced the floor, trying to create new ideas for escaping, but nothing came. Instead of coming up with something new, she relived, moment by moment, everything that had happened since Tenley and Jake had abducted her Saturday morning.

Stacey paused by the window. The rain had stopped. Far down the road, a couple of kids pedaled bicycles, and she envied their freedom. Her thoughts churned back to her imprisonment. Suddenly she whirled, diving for the wastebasket. When Neva untied her, she'd thrown the strips of sheet in there. Maybe she could get away after all—as soon as it was dark.

The strips were gone. Neva must have taken them out while she was in the shower. Her spirits sank even lower than before.

She picked up the tray, sat on the bed and balanced it across her knees. Listlessly eating the sandwich, Stacey hardly tasted it or the crisp vegetables.

While still eating, she heard sounds in the drive below. She listened. It wasn't a car, but it had wheels. They grated against the gravel.

"I'll do the talking," said a young voice.

"Okay."

Stacey slumped back against the headboard. Just kids. Probably the two on bikes. But she found herself trying to hear, all the same. When they knocked on the door, Jake hollered, "Get away. Didn't you see the 'no trespassing' signs? You're on private property."

"But, sir," said the spokesman. "We're trying to—"

"I don't care what you're trying to do. Get out!"

"But, sir," the boy repeated.

That's a brave kid, thought Stacey, *to stand up to Jake. I'm surprised he hasn't thrown them down the road, bikes and all.*

"We're returning this. Thought it might belong to you."

"My card folder. Where'd you get it?"

Card folder. The leather case she'd dropped.

"We found it out in the woods south of town. Sorry it's so dirty. It was in a mud puddle."

After a brief silence, the other boy said, "We didn't take nothin', Mister. We only looked inside to get this address so we could return it."

Stacey groaned. Her one clue, now gone. She set aside the tray and walked to the window, wanting to see the boys who'd wrecked her last hope of being rescued.

There were two of them, one with carrot red hair, the other with hair as black as her own. They were already on their bikes, headed down the lane. The door slammed below, and both boys turned to look back. Frantically she waved, trying to catch their attention without yelling and gaining Jake's anger.

She thought one boy nudged the other, but they pedaled off.

The disappointment was too much. Stacey slammed the tray onto the dresser and flung herself on the bed. She was helpless and could do nothing to make things right.

Stacey lay on her back and stared at the ceiling. One of wo things would happen. Either her dad would turn his message over to the spies and that new democratic leader would be assassinated, or he'd get the word through to the proper authorities and . . . and what? Would they turn her loose? Make other plans?

To carry out an assassination would be harder when the man was alerted and could protect himself. Would they . . . would they kill her or take their anger out on her family? Maybe kill them all?

Stacey brushed her hands across her face to try to wipe out such morbid, hopeless thoughts, but they persisted until finally she fell asleep. She dreamed of being chased over narrow rock paths with stone walls on one side and deep chasms on the other.

She awoke at the sound of the door and looked up as dinner was carried in. After she ate, they allowed her another shower. Stacey was glad for the opportunity to get out of her cramped little room. Then the sun set and darkness hid the ugly view. For a long time, she stared at the night sky, wishing for the friendliness of a twinkling star, but clouds blocked the stars from view.

Another day gone. What would tomorrow bring?

Stacey curled up under the blanket and lay quietly. She was more aware than ever of the silence of the house. It was hard to believe at least five other people were hidden inside its walls. The only sounds she had ever heard from within were Jake's occasional bellows at her and footsteps on the stairs.

Even outside it was quiet. Occasionally the sound of a car droned in the distance. A couple of times planes flew over, but after the birds quieted for the night, the country air was silent.

She must have dozed, for all of a sudden she was wide awake. She'd heard something. The noise came from outside. There it was again—a small thud, followed by a muted scrape, then a rustling and almost imperceptible squeaking.

A darker shadow rose against the blackness of her window. A soft tap, tap sounded as the shadow moved.

She flung off the blanket and crept to the window. She unfastened the lock and pushed up the pane.

"Stacey?"

"Yes."

"I'm Alex Nelson," a voice whispered. "Can you climb down a ladder?"

"I can do anything to get out of here."

"I'll start down. Let me get halfway before you get on the ladder. But hurry." Alex disappeared.

Stacey padded to the bed, fumbling for her shoes. She didn't take time to tie them, just slid them on her feet and hurried back to the window. She leaned out, holding her breath. Alex was at the bottom, motioning frantically for her to hurry. She swung herself onto the window ledge and twisted around, her feet groping for a rung.

Steady on the ladder, she reached up to try to close the window.

"Don't bother with that. Someone could come out any minute!" The hoarse whisper seemed to shriek in Stacey's ears. She scampered down the ladder.

"Run," Alex ordered. "When you get to the road, turn left."

Stacey wondered why left when town was to the right, but she didn't argue. Taking time only to tie her shoes, she set off down the lane. She'd barely cleared the yard when Alex and his friend Harry caught up with her, carrying the ladder still stretched full length.

The boys ran in perfect unison, somehow skirting the potholes and rocks that made her stumble and almost fall.

"Hsst." Alex motioned toward the ladder. "Grab on. It makes it easier. Just keep in step with Harry."

Stacey followed his whispered instructions and had less trouble. When they reached the main road, they paused. Harry and Alex telescoped the extension ladder back to its shortest size. The sound of metal sliding on metal echoed on the night air.

Stacey looked back at the house that had been her prison

for the past three days. It remained pitch dark. Not a light visible anywhere. She shuddered, hoping she'd never see it again.

"Ready?" Alex questioned, motioning down the road. "We're not in the clear yet."

"Ready," Stacey answered.

They started at a jog, the two boys carrying the shortened ladder, Stacey moving between them. After the house was out of sight, they slowed to a fast walk.

"How'd you find me?" Stacey asked, breathing hard.

"Easy." Harry grinned back at her. "Me and Alex just followed the clues, and there you were."

"I only left one." Stacey brushed the hair out of her eyes. "And that one fizzled."

"What was it?" Alex asked.

"I managed to drop a card case that was sticking out of Jake's back pocket when he carried me through the woods. I didn't think I had very high hopes of anyone finding it. It fell in a mud puddle. But when a couple of boys returned it this morning, I thought my last chance had disappeared. Especially when the boys seemed to see my waving and just left anyway."

Alex chuckled.

Stacey twisted to look back at him. "It wasn't funny," she snapped, then stopped. Something about the look on Alex's face made her catch her breath. "It wasn't you?"

"Yup. Just scouting the place."

"But one of those boys had flaming red hair. The other—"

Harry laughed. "Mom's old wigs outta the attic. At first I didn't want to wear the silly thing, but Alex is right. The guy who answered the door will never recognize us again. They really made us look different."

Ahead on the right of the road, Stacey saw the lights of a convenience store. "Is that where we're headed?"

"Yeah. Got a phone call to make."

Alex motioned them off the road, across the ditch and

into a field. Stealthily they crept toward the back of the store.

When they were about a hundred yards away, Alex signaled a stop, dropping the ladder flat on the ground. "Stacey, you wait here. Harry and I'll go in and call. Whatever happens, just hang tough. Don't move. If a car drives up, flatten out on the ladder so no one will see you."

The two boys left her sitting on the ladder. They walked back the way they'd come, then swaggered up the road.

For a few minutes, Stacey sat, quietly amused that these two young teens had done what the CIA had been unable to do. She stretched her arms out and up, enjoying her freedom. It was wonderful. Thank goodness for two mystery-addicted boys.

Stacey glanced at her watch. She couldn't see in the darkness. The lights from the store didn't penetrate this far. They'd been gone a long time. Should she go after them?

No, Alex had been very explicit. She was to stay put. But it was hard to sit and wait when she wanted desperately to hurry home and tell her parents she was safe, that her dad didn't have to jeopardize the life of that African leader.

She had just stood up to pace back and forth, when headlights from a racing car cut through the darkness. The tires squealed as the driver slammed on the brakes and cut into the parking area. The doors flung open and two men jumped out. Charlie and Jake.

Stacey sank to the ground, glad the boys had insisted she stay behind. She lay on the horribly uncomfortable rungs of the ladder, holding her breath, though there was no possible way they could hear her.

Would Alex and Harry be all right? Had the wigs been good enough disguises? Did Charlie and Jake know who they were?

Peering through the weeds, Stacey saw the boys come out of the store. She could hear Jake's booming voice.

"Hey, kids. You seen a girl around here? About five-six, black hair?"

"How old?" Alex asked.

"Eighteen or nineteen."

"Did she run away?" That was Harry. Bless their hearts. Besides being detectives, they were consummate actors.

"No." Charlie sounded worried. "She's had a nervous breakdown. Wanders off. Doesn't know where or even who she is. Has delusions of persecution."

If Stacey weren't the girl in question, she might have believed the sincerity in his voice.

"Yeah." Jake's voice broke in on Charlie's. "She's in a bad way."

"We haven't seen anyone except the people in the store. No one like that in there."

"How long you been here?"

"Just long enough to call our folks and tell them we'd lost our ride and would be late." Alex hunched his shoulders. "You know how parents worry over the least little thing."

"Yeah. Which way'd you come?" Jake demanded.

"Up the road."

Stacey marveled. Harry's answer hadn't been explicit, yet both Jake and Charlie looked off in the wrong direction.

"Hope you find your daughter," Alex said. He and Harry started trudging toward town. The two men stared after them.

Jake scratched his head. "Hey, kids. Want a lift into town? We're going that way."

"Thanks, but Dad's on his way. We told him we'd start walking."

The two men turned and walked into the store. Less than a minute later, they slammed out, jumped into their car and roared off toward town.

Chapter Sixteen

Questions darted at Stacey. How had Jake and Charlie known she was gone? They hadn't come to her room this late at night before. Was something wrong?

Stacey breathed a thanks to God that the boys had come when they did and they'd gotten away. What if the boys had come half an hour later? She shuddered at the thought of how narrowly she'd escaped.

She rose to her knees and watched as the car raced toward town, then jammed on its brakes, the red lights brilliant in the darkness.

Against the gleam of the headlights, she saw two figures move to the car, hesitate, then cross back over the road. Jake gunned the engine and the car disappeared around a curve.

Stacey could no longer see the boys. Were they coming across the field? She strained her eyes in the darkness to no avail. Faint music drifted from the convenience store, but no other sounds broke the silence of the night—no indication of the boys returning.

Minutes lengthened and dragged. Stacey paced back and forth, keeping a wary eye on the road. A couple of cars passed heading toward town. Each time she dropped to her knees.

Still no sign of the boys. Surely they wouldn't leave her. Were they afraid Jake and Charlie would come back? She wished they'd come and wait with her. She hated not knowing what was going on. Besides, she was getting cold, and her clothes, wet from the rain-washed grass, began to feel clammy.

She ducked again as a couple of cars drove by, headed out of town. One drove on up the road, the other stopped at the store. Could that be Alex's dad already?

Huddled on the ladder, Stacey watched to see if someone would come around back. But in a few moments, the car took off up the road again.

A hand touched her shoulder. She gasped and whirled, sliding off the rung of the ladder, landing in the soaking grass.

"Sorry, didn't mean to frighten you. Thought you'd hear us coming." Alex's voice was a mere murmur of sound.

"What took you so long?" she whispered back.

"Didn't dare leave the road until a car came out from town. Those two guys would be suspicious if they came back and found us gone when they hadn't met a car. We didn't want to take chances."

Stacey shivered. "Is your dad really coming?"

"No. He's in Boston, visiting Mom."

Her heart dropped. How would they get to town?

"I didn't dare take time to look up your number, so I called Mike. He and Ken should be on their way."

Stacey's heart skipped a beat. Ken. He was all right and on his way.

"We'd better get going," Harry put in. "We don't want to miss them."

"Right." Alex picked up the ladder. Harry grabbed the other end and they started off. "We'll skirt on around the store and head up the road. There's a side road about half a mile from here where I told them to meet us.

The action warmed Stacey. She had gotten chilled waiting so long, and it was good to be moving again. When they turned off into the intersecting street, she was almost sorry. The boys stopped, setting down the ladder.

"Where did you get that ladder, anyway?" she asked. "Did you carry it all the way from town?"

"We, uh, sort of borrowed it," Harry stammered.

"We noticed it lying out beside a fence at the next house down the road from where you were. It was just the ticket. So, we used it."

"We'll drop it back where we found it on the way home," Harry promised. "The owner will probably never know it was moved."

"How did you find me? How did you know that the folder had anything to do with me?"

Harry hunched his shoulders against the cold. "We saw you."

"What?"

"We were in the woods that morning. We'd biked out to do some exploring."

Alex took up the story. "We'd just found an ideal . . . er . . . an ideal spot for what we wanted, when we saw you walking out with those two guys." He shook his head. "We thought you were in cahoots with them somehow. You didn't even try to get away. Just walked along like you were friends."

"Ken was back in the woods." Stacey shuddered, remembering. "We'd been bird watching and taking pictures. They'd beat him up already and threatened to go back and kill him if I tried to yell or escape."

"Yeah, you'd have to go along," Harry said after considering her story. "It'd be the only thing you could do."

"Well, we rode on into the woods, hoping to find an even better situation than the one close to the entrance." Alex motioned for silence, listened intently for a minute, then went on. "We were doing wheelies and things with our bikes, hitting the mud puddles."

"That's how we happened to find the card case. You should have seen it. He had quite a selection of cards. All different names and occupations. That's pretty shady."

Alex grinned. "We didn't know if it belonged to one of

the guys with you or not. You hadn't mentioned anyone named Jake or Jason or Jasper or James—those were some of the names on the cards—that night at the Shanty. But we knew it hadn't been in the puddle long. The cards weren't soaked yet.

"Why didn't you come out Saturday?"

"For a couple of reasons," Harry said. "We had to make plans, to decide whether this had anything to do with your mystery. Besides, we didn't know you'd been kidnapped. We thought you went on your own."

"That's right. I was staying over at Harry's for the weekend, so it wasn't until I got home Sunday night that I learned that you were missing. Erica, Mike, Ken and that whole bunch were frantic."

"Spent all their time praying," put in Harry. "We decided action was necessary."

"Knowing you'd been kidnapped made the card case real evidence. We called your house. A woman called Miriam answered and said she was a friend of your mother's; that you couldn't come to the phone." Alex snorted in disgust. "When we told her we possibly had some evidence that might help find you, she told us to quit playing practical kid jokes. Some friend."

Harry paced a few steps back and forth. "We got the idea she might have been one of the kidnappers, holding your mother, too."

"She's a CIA agent," Stacey said. "She moved in a few days ago to protect us."

"Hah! Some protection," Harry scoffed.

"No. It was my fault." Stacey got up to walk with Harry. "I wasn't supposed to go anywhere alone. I thought I'd be safe with Ken out in the woods so early in the morning. I went without telling them. Just left a note."

Neither boy said anything to make her feel it was a dumb thing to do. She sighed with gratitude.

"Ken . . . Ken is all right, isn't he?"

"He's got a real beaut of a bruise on his jaw. Otherwise

he's fine." Alex still sprawled on the ladder. "When we couldn't get any help, we decided we'd have to do it ourselves. We biked out here and returned the case. Boy, am I glad you finally showed up at that window. I thought we'd blown our only excuse for hanging around without finding out a thing!"

"Why didn't you wave back?"

Harry's voice sounded disgusted. "There're windows downstairs, too. Didn't know who might be watching us. Couldn't jeopardize the whole plan just to let you know we'd seen you."

"Quick. Back in the bushes." Alex and Harry grabbed the ladder and plunged into the young alders that lined the road. "Hurry," Alex urged.

Stacey followed, the young branches whipping her cold shoulders and arms. Hidden in the dense foliage, she peered out. Headlights illuminated the spot where they'd been talking. The car stopped.

"Wait another minute," Alex warned. "It's Mike's car, but let's be sure no one followed them."

After a moment, the car doors swung open and the two young men stepped out.

"Alex?" Mike called. "Alex? Are you here?"

Motioning the other two to remain where they were, Alex swished through the trees and jumped the ditch to the road. "Right here. You guys alone?"

"Yeah. What's the big mystery? How'd you get out here without a way home?"

"Got a surprise for you." Alex motioned with his arm.

Harry picked up one end of the ladder. "Help me with this, will you?"

Stacey picked up the other end and walked out onto the road.

"Stacey!" Ken reached her in one leap. He threw his arms around her, pulling her to him.

She dropped the ladder and put her arms around him. "Oh, Ken. I'm so sorry. Are you all right?"

"Of course." He held her away from him, looking at her for a long moment. "Are *you* okay?"

"Now. Since you're here. Oh, Ken, I'm so glad to see you."

He pulled her close again, then noticed the other three grinning at them. "Let's get her home. Her parents will want to see her as soon as possible."

"Shall we stop at the store and call them?" Mike asked, getting back into the car.

"No," chorused Alex and Harry.

"A couple of kidnappers were there not too long ago."

Alex climbed in the back seat with Harry. "The house they kept her in is just down the road. Let's get out of here."

Ken helped Stacey into the front seat. He put his arm around her shoulders, pulled her close. "You're shivering. Cold?"

"A little. It was wet out there in the grass. But mostly I think it's relief. I'm so glad to be free." She snuggled close to him, drawing warmth and comfort from his presence.

Mike looked into the back seat. "Do we have to go past that place? Is there another way to town?"

"Yeah." Harry pointed in the opposite direction. "About five miles up the road there's a cut-off that'll take us the long way around. We come out four miles east on Highway 2."

Mike nodded and started the engine.

"Wait, we forgot the ladder. We've got to return it." Alex leaned forward. "I don't want to have stolen it."

The boys piled out of the car and picked up the ladder. "How are we going to carry it? It won't fit in the trunk."

"We could just hold it out the window," Harry suggested.

"Let's come back for it tomorrow," suggested Ken. "If you used that thing to help Stacey escape and we go driving down the road with it hanging off the car, we're a dead giveaway."

"Right." Alex maneuvered the ladder until it was hidden

in the trees, then climbed in the car.

Within a half hour, they were pulling up at the White home. Everything was pitch black. *One-thirty*, thought Stacey. She wondered if her parents were sleeping or if they were out looking for her. Was her dad even now giving his classified information to the enemy?

"Let's go," she whispered, not knowing why. "I want to see Mom. Dad, too, if he's here."

"He's here. Flew in Saturday." Ken sat still. "I think you'd better stay here until we're sure everything's all right. Let me go to the door first."

Ken let himself out, closing the door quietly. Stacey watched him walk to the door, pause, then ring the bell. He rang a second time. Lights flashed on in her parent's room and the guest room where Miriam was staying.

The porch light flared, and then the front door opened a fraction. Stacey couldn't hear the words, but the door was jerked inward and her mom and dad started down the steps. She flung herself out of the car and raced to meet them.

They both grabbed her at the same time and she threw her arms around them. "Mom. Dad. I'm so sorry. I didn't mean to cause you so much worry."

"Darling." Mrs. White whispered through tears. "It's so wonderful to see you. Are you all right?

With one arm still around Stacey, Mr. White reached out and clasped Ken's shoulder. "Thank you, son. I don't know where you found her, but we're grateful."

"I'm only along for the ride. Alex and Harry are the heroes."

Mrs. White retied the belt on her dressing gown and walked to the car, tears falling down her face. Bending over to see through the windows, she invited, "Come on in, boys. We want to thank you for what you've done."

They scrambled out of the car, with Mike following.

"Quick," Miriam prodded. "Give me some information." She asked questions about the farm house, the number of people. "Got to get some agents out there, before they all disappear. They won't hang around long with you gone."

"They think Stacey jumped and is hiding in the woods," Alex offered. "We heard Jake and Charlie talking. They're sure she must have at least sprained something jumping and can't be far away."

Miriam smiled her thanks and rushed to the phone.

Over hot chocolate and cookies, the boys retold the story of how they'd followed their clues and rescued Stacey.

When Stacey had told her part of the story, she looked at her dad. "Dad, are you really a courier for the CIA?"

He looked at Miriam, who nodded. "Well, I was. Only when I was already scheduled to be where a drop needed to be made." He grinned. "I guess that part of my life is over. Since I've been spotted, I won't be of much use to them any more."

"Dad! You enjoyed it."

He smiled at her. "Surprise you?"

She grinned back. "Not really. Not once I started thinking it could be possible. You'd agree first because you thought it was your duty. Then I remembered all the spy novels you liked to read. I tried to keep that memory hidden, though, so Neva and Tenley wouldn't see that I'd decided you could be a courier."

Mrs. White stared at them. "I had no idea. How long?"

"Several years." He patted his wife's shoulder. "They only gave me assignments that held little risk. I've never been in real danger."

"Dad, are you the courier for the information about the assassination of the African leader?"

He nodded. "Yes. It was delivered over two weeks ago."

"But nothing happened. Charlie said they were sure that it hadn't gotten through because no activity had taken place. That was the purpose of this whole thing."

"The leader to be assassinated felt he had a far better chance of catching his enemies if no word got out that he was warned. If they thought they were still safe, they'd make the attempt. He could not only save his life, but also end the plot and not have to worry about this particular bunch in the future."

The ringing of the phone cut into his explanation. Miriam reached to answer. She listened for a moment.

"All of them? Evidence? Good. Wait a minute." Miriam put her hand over the receiver. "Stacey, they're asking about an older woman. She claims she lives there and had nothing to do with the kidnapping."

"Jake's mother. Have them leave her alone. She was kind to me, fixed special meals and gave me roses. She's afraid of Jake. He'd beat her up if she didn't do what he said."

Miriam relayed the information to the other agents and hung up. "I guess that's that. They're all in custody."

Mrs. White stood. "Then I think we should all get to bed. I know I'm about to drop."

The boys scrambled to their feet. "Thanks for the chocolate," Alex said.

"Yeah," agreed Harry. "It was great."

Mr. White put a hand on each boy's shoulder. "I don't know how to thank you boys. You've done something for us that is beyond repayment. We're deeply grateful, more than you'll ever know. If there's anything you want—"

"Uh, it's all right, Mr. White. We were glad to do it." Alex smiled. "We like solving mysteries."

"Yeah. We had fun. But . . ."

"Yes?" Mr. White prompted.

"Sometime, if it's okay, we'd like to see your lab. Look at all the stuff you're working on."

"I think we can arrange that. I'll be here for the rest of the week. Come in Thursday or Friday. Okay?"

"You bet." Both boys headed for the door, followed by Mike and Mr. and Mrs. White. Miriam headed up to bed.

Ken and Stacey lingered in the kitchen. "I'm awfully glad you're okay," Ken murmured in her ear. "I've been blaming myself for taking you out Saturday morning when my better judgment told me I should return you to the house."

"I should never have asked you. But I wanted that last fling at freedom." She blushed as she looked up and confessed, "I wanted to be alone with you. I think I've learned a little about obedience through this. It'll be a while before I insist on having my own way."

"A tough way to learn a lesson."

A frown creased Stacey's forehead. "For a while, I thought Charlie might decide for the Lord. Last Friday night, I gave him my New Testament and he seemed interested. That's when he decided to try to save me."

"And?"

"The first night at the farm house, he gave it back. I was glad to have it. It helped pass a lot of hours and gave me peace and hope, but I felt awful about Charlie. He'd made his decision. It was for money."

"Maybe now that he won't be getting it, and with time to think, he'll remember and consider. God will work. We can pray for that."

Ken drew Stacey into his arms. "I've only a minute left. You've got to get out of those damp clothes and get some sleep."

"I'm not cold any more. But I guess I am tired." She snuggled against him. "I'm glad you were along when Mike came."

"Me, too. I knew from the first moment I saw you in the woods that you were someone special, but these past three days have shown me how much I really care."

Stacey looked up into his eyes, her own sparkling. "You're the first person ever to tell me that. The first person I've wanted to feel that way." She reached up and put her arms around him.

He kissed her gently, then propelled her into the hall where the others were waiting.

"Ready?" Mike asked.

"Yeah." Ken turned back to Stacey. "See you Thursday night?"

Standing between her parents, arms entwined with both, she glanced at them for their approval. Then she nodded. "I'll be there."